"Miss Bell!"

Lord Hastings's forceful voice commanded Felicity's attention.

"I will escort you in this ill-advised pursuit of your sister because I am averse to reading about your untimely demise in the *Gazette*! But never, never offer me money again! Not even a half-penny! Do you understand?"

"Yes," she answered softly but promptly.

"And," he added, "if you should cause me the least inconvenience on this trip, if you prove to be too wilful to tolerate, I shall leave you at whatever dwelling we should happen to be passing at the time."

"Agreed!" Felicity said at last, then turned her back and exited the room in a flurry of blue muslin.

Vastly enjoying his leverage over Miss Bell, Lord Hastings called out in his most ⬚⬚⬚⬚⬚⬚ ⬚ice, "Aren't you staying to tak⬚ ⬚⬚⬚⬚⬚⬚

"I shall eat in m⬚ ⬚⬚⬚⬚⬚⬚⬚⬚⬚⬚⬚⬚⬚⬚⬚⬚rt.

Lord Hastings ⬚⬚⬚⬚⬚⬚⬚⬚⬚⬚⬚⬚⬚⬚⬚⬚⬚⬚⬚lf into?

Books by Emily Dalton

HARLEQUIN REGENCY ROMANCE
31–A COUNTRY CHIT
44–AN INFAMOUS SEA BATH

Don't miss any of our special offers. Write to us at the
following address for information on our newest releases.

Harlequin Reader Service
P.O. Box 1397, Buffalo, NY 14240
Canadian address: P.O. Box 603,
Fort Erie, Ont. L2A 5X3

BEAUTY AND THE BEASTIE

EMILY DALTON

Harlequin Books

TORONTO • NEW YORK • LONDON
AMSTERDAM • PARIS • SYDNEY • HAMBURG
STOCKHOLM • ATHENS • TOKYO • MILAN

Dedicated to my Mom, Lorena Ford,
from whom I inherited a fanciful mind.

"To see her is to love her,
    And love but her for ever,
For Nature made her what she is,
    And ne'er made anither!"
                                    —Robert Burns

Published October 1991

ISBN 0-373-31159-1

BEAUTY AND THE BEASTIE

CHAPTER ONE

"FELICITY! NEVER SAY you're travelling to Scotland quite alone! Dearest child, it just isn't done! I'm your paid companion, as well as your relative, and it is my *duty* to accompany you! What will your brother say?"

Aunt Mathilda's plaintive voice had a distinctly nasal tone. She'd been abed for the past four days with a violent cold. Now she stood in Felicity's bedchamber in her nightdress, pressing a handkerchief soaked in camphorated spirits of lavender to her red and swollen nose. She had a roasted onion stuffed in one afflicted ear, secured by a bandage tied round her head, and a mustard plaster was applied liberally to her narrow spinster's chest. She smelled as wretched as she looked.

"Dearest Aunt!" exclaimed Felicity, shoving her tooth-powder into a large, embroidered reticule. "Firstly, I'm not a child and am well able to take care of myself. And, in good conscience, I could not drag you from your sickbed for any reason, least of all to lend propriety to a mad dash to Gretna Green! Secondly, we are so near the border here I do not imagine that I shall be gone above a day or two. I hoped this whole affair involving my sister might be kept a secret from those who would gleefully do harm with the information. And thirdly, I don't care a fig for Henry's opinion!''

''Miss?'' interjected a chambermaid, holding up two dresses. ''You said I was only to pack two travelling gowns. Will these do?''

''The blue will do nicely, but I feel an absolute dowdy in grey. I wonder where it came from? I'm quite certain *I* didn't have it made! Probably another of Henry's gifts,'' she observed consideringly. ''Put it away and pack my rose sarcenet, will you, Chloe?''

''Felicity, you are much too apt to wear colours that, er, clash with your titian hair!'' scolded her aunt from behind the folds of her handkerchief. ''Even the apple green you're wearing now is much too vivid!''

''Don't you mean to say that I wear colours as bright as my hair, the combination of which border on the vulgar? Do not scruple to tell me so, Aunt Tilda. Henry frequently does! And so does my abigail. The poor dear!''

''What do you mean, 'the poor dear'!'' exclaimed Aunt Mathilda, darting a quick look about the large, sunlit room. ''Where is your abigail, Felicity? Should she not be helping pack?''

''Indeed I'm sure she would be if she weren't—''

''Packing her own bag, I suppose,'' interrupted Aunt Mathilda hopefully.

"Knocked up with a putrid sore throat and taken to her bed," finished Felicity.

"You intend to go to Scotland without even your abigail?" the elderly woman rasped as she painfully inhaled. "Felicity, your reputation will be beyond repair if you persist in this wilful behaviour! Genteel Society will shun you!"

Aunt Mathilda might have continued with her direful predictions, but she was compelled to stop and blow her nose, the resulting goose-like sound requiring the chambermaid to stifle a giggle.

Felicity paused in her own preparations for the trip and smiled wryly at her aunt. "You might be of use in sounding our arrival at the toll-gates and inn-yards, I daresay, Aunt Tilda. But Hugo does so like his yard of tin!"

"This is not the time for one of your witticisms, Felicity!" reproved her aunt. "Susan has got herself into the devil of a coil, the naughty child! How I wish she'd stayed safe at home with us! What could she possibly see in Lieutenant Kennedy which would make her do such a ramshackle thing as jilt Wenthorp and run off to Gretna Green?"

"I can think of any number of reasons for jilting Wenthorp," stated Felicity.

"Henry says Wenthorp is eminently suitable!" argued her aunt.

"But rather prosy and boring, much like Henry," Felicity answered flatly, as she placed her bonnet over her mass of burnished curls. "I've often wondered if Susan accepted Wenthorp merely to avoid another Season. Everything about the Town seemed to upset her nerves—the noise, the crowds, the impertinent stares. But whenever I broached the subject, she refused to be drawn into conversation.''

"But still, I do not understand why she is so smitten with the lieutenant!''

"As for Lieutenant Kennedy,'' continued Felicity, recalled to her original subject. "He is very charming and excessively good-looking. His Scottish lilt is beguiling. And that time when Susan tripped on her demi-train at Helen Starkey's ball and the lieutenant caught her in his arms, I'm quite sure Susan's heart was all aflutter. Though, heaven knows, since we've come to London any number of men have been required to intervene between dear clumsy Susan and the floor!''

"Yes, the child's feet seem constantly in a tangle,'' clucked Aunt Mathilda.

"It was not so in Yorkshire, Aunt Tilda,'' Felicity pointed out. "Only when Susan is nervous does she turn into a positive clodpole! Otherwise, she is quite graceful!''

Felicity moved to stand in front of a long cheval glass. "The lieutenant's attentions towards her were excessive, despite the fact he was told time and again that she was betrothed to another! It is regrettable for Wenthorp that he was summoned home by his possessive mama to Hertfordshire, though I doubt not Lieutenant Kennedy would have flirted with Susan right under her fiancé's nose none the less. The lieutenant seems a determined, passionate fellow. Timid, sensitive Susan would be no proof against such ardour! He would either frighten her to death or make her fall head over ears in love with him. I suspect—I hope!—he accomplished the last!'' But Felicity would not be satisfied until she knew for sure.

Unimpressed by this list of attractions, Aunt Mathilda said, ''But must he always wear a kilt? A man's bare legs somehow seem shocking in Polite Society!'' She shuddered.

''He's Scottish, Aunt Tilda!'' replied Felicity, laughing.

''And he's too tall! I cannot abide a too-tall man, Felicity!''

''I've no objection to the young man's height,'' replied Felicity. ''Since there are so few men who are equal to the prospect of standing up for a set of dances with such a long meg as myself, his height actually makes me more in sympathy with the fellow. But, I agree—for once!—with Henry that given the rapidity of their budding romance, Susan needed to be removed from London and away from Lieutenant Kennedy's charms until we knew something more of his family and situation in life. Since Henry needs must stay in London till little Emma's tooth is pulled, it seemed logical that I bring Susan ahead to Yorkshire with me.''

"A pity the lieutenant was not more forward in talking about himself," said Aunt Mathilda, her voice muted as she snuffled into her handkerchief.

"Yes, but that may have been owing to his complete absorption in Susan. I want to believe the best of him. Having been an officer in His Majesty's Highlander Troops who only just returned from the victory at Waterloo is admirable. But, while he seems a right enough fellow, appearances can be deceiving. For all we know, his family could be deep in dun territory and on the look-out for an advantageous match. We must never forget that Susan is an heiress and, as such, in need of protection from fortune-hunters! I could not bear Susan to be taken advantage of in such a way!"

"Susan resented your suspicions of Lieutenant Kennedy's intentions, Felicity," her aunt informed her with a sage nod.

"Yes, I know, Aunt Tilda," sighed Felicity. "But they were not suspicions, really. I was simply suggesting caution as any older sister would do. But it seems that all we've accomplished by separating them is to force them into this elopement, which was really quite unnecessary. Unless, of course, the lieutenant has something to hide!"

"Are you sure you can catch them up? You and the servants were away at church for more than two hours, giving them quite a lead. If only I hadn't been sleeping so soundly, I might have heard them leave and somehow sent word to you!"

Felicity finished tying her bonnet ribbands and stared thoughtfully into the mirror reflecting her aunt's thin, distraught face. She pursed her lips and considered the matter further. "'Tis true that if Susan packed her bags last night when she went early to bed with the headache—the minx!—Lieutenant Kennedy need only have waited till our carriages were through the gate this morning to collect his beloved. When I looked in on her after breakfast and she pleaded herself too ill to go to church, I thought she looked rather feverish. Now I know the true source of her agitation!"

Then she patted her copper curls and said, in a brisker, brighter tone, "But even so, if we ride hellbent for leather we'll have caught up with them in the twinkling of a bedpost! I'm quite sure that one, perhaps two, nights in an inn is all that will be required."

"I wish I were as sanguine as you," Aunt Mathilda observed doubtfully. "But instead, I am beset with spasms and palpitations! After all, I'm an old woman and not accustomed to all this helter-skelter behaviour! If it were my decision, I should place the whole matter in the hands of your capable brother!"

"By the time I sent word to London, Susan would be married and the union consummated! I've no recourse but to follow her immediately!"

Aunt Mathilda blushed at the word "consummated," spoken with such nonchalance by her niece, but the urgency of the matter seemed finally to have struck her.

"And you, Aunt Tilda, must go back to bed! It was good of you to see me off but now I really must go!" Felicity firmly insisted. She put her arm round the diminutive woman and escorted her back to her room. Tucking her aunt snugly in her bed, Felicity ordered another hot brick to place at her chilled feet, as all the while the elderly woman muttered feeble objections. Then Felicity kissed her on the forehead and said, "I'm leaving you in good hands. You know what an excellent nurse Mrs. Cummings is. I wonder she isn't up here now fussing about!"

"She's probably stewing a chicken," returned her aunt with a petulant sniff.

"She does have her duties, you know," reasoned Felicity. "And mayhap the stewed chicken is broth for your soup, dearest!" Then, in the kind but firm tone she was compelled to use with her aunt, "Now remember, dear, do not, under any inducement, send word of this escapade to Henry. And Wenthorp particularly must be kept in the dark. I don't think he's got the pluck to kick up a dust, but we cannot be too sure! I shall deal with the situation and have the whole matter under control in no time. If there is any delay I shall write to you. And if the vicar or some other neighbour should call, tell them Susan and I have gone to visit a friend."

"Such managing behaviour is unnatural in a woman, Felicity," said her aunt, her eyes drooping

sleepily. "Just goes to show what happens to a
woman in complete command of her own fortune
and without the restraint or assistance of a father, or
some other male relative... Like a husband, perhaps...."

Aunt Mathilda's voice faded and presently Felicity discerned the whine of a stuffy nose endeavouring to snore. She smiled, gave her aunt one last pat
on her capped head and left the room.

*Well, if Henry must thrust a companion on me, at
least it was someone as dear and harmless as Aunt
Mathilda,* thought Felicity as she hurried down the
hall to her own bedchamber. In fact, if she'd known
before how straitened her aunt's circumstances were,
she'd have invited her to live with her much sooner.
As it was, everyone was made happier by the arrangement. Henry had procured a companion to put
a proper face on Felicity's eccentric penchant for
living alone, her aunt was provided with a more
comfortable home, and Felicity was still able to do
precisely as she pleased.

Like a small bantam hen, her aunt fluttered about,
dutifully cajoling, complaining and lecturing in an
effort to justify her comfortable existence at Heathwood Manor, her niece's residence on the outskirts
of the village of Thirsk in Yorkshire. Felicity's father had been the local squire of the area, and now
Henry held that distinction.

But despite Aunt Mathilda's efforts, at five-and-
twenty Felicity was too set in her ways to be much

influenced by anyone. If only Henry could be convinced that she was as capable as any man to manage her own affairs! But her father's dying plea to Henry that he watch over his two sisters was taken very much to his eldest son's heart.

Possessed of her own considerable fortune, Felicity had stoutly refused Henry's invitation to live with him and his large family when her father died. She was determined not to be relegated to the pathetic position of resident maiden aunt, forever obliged to be pleasant and useful. Felicity had much rather live alone and plan her days and evenings to suit herself. The house she leased was only a mile away from Henry's, and she visited them often and they her, which arrangement she found much more agreeable than forever being under one anothers' noses.

If some of the local tittle-tattles privately raised their brows and whispered about Felicity's singular situation, at least Henry's high and respectable position in the community prevented them from voicing overly loud their disapproval.

Since Susan was a child of only thirteen at the time of her parent's death and Henry was her legal guardian, there was no question that she must remain in residence with him. Despite living in separate households, Felicity strove to stay as close to Susan as possible. Her sister's timid nature seemed to bring out Felicity's protective instincts. She was used to watching out for Susan.

Felicity hurriedly finished her preparations for the trip. Moments later she was leaving the tidy yards which surrounded her neat Yorkshire house, waving and smiling reassuringly at Mrs. Cummings and Richards, the butler, who bade her farewell from the front steps.

Presently, she leaned back against the squabs of her well-sprung carriage and watched through the window as they passed through the quiet village of Thirsk. The usually busy shops were closed for the Sabbath, except for the Golden Fleece coaching house and taproom which was always open for the thirsty wanderer. Lastly, they passed St. Oswald's church, where she'd attended services that very morning. Now she deeply regretted her invitation to Vicar Sowerby to come for tea. She hoped he did not plan to avail himself of her hospitality in the too-near future.

Finally they were in the open countryside where the gentle rush of the Codbeck could be heard flowing alongside the road, and the imposing ridge of the Hambletons loomed in the distance. Thank goodness they'd not be compelled to travel over the mountains, just round them.

But a glance at the sky left her feeling a little less sanguine. A previously clear aspect of the heavens had clouded over since the morning. Were they in for some inclement weather? Felicity hoped not. Since it was early June and the days were long, and Hugo had indeed set a spanking pace, she felt reasonably sure they'd catch up with the miscreants before nightfall—even should they encounter a little rain.

THE COACH HOBBLED into the muddy inn-yard under the siege of a torrential storm. Hugo had blown his yard of tin and a thin, shadowy form appeared at the narrow entrance to the inn, stretching out a single dim lantern into the murky darkness.

Felicity hadn't the slightest idea where they were. In the low glow of the carriage lamplight, she observed the hands of her watch-locket. It was just going on to eight o'clock, but it was already too dark to read the inn's name, declared, as it were, on a large sign above the door. No matter. She was willing at this point to tolerate even the crudest accommodations to be relieved of the close confines of her carriage! She opened the window to speak to the shadow in the doorway.

"My good man, is there anyone able to lend my coachman a hand with my bag, and an ostler for the horses?" she enquired.

"Yes'm! Right away, mum!" answered the man at the door, obviously noting the ring of Quality in Felicity's voice. After sending a smaller figure out into the rain to attend to the horses, he personally assisted Felicity from the carriage. His escort, however, did not save her from sinking her lovely nankeen boots nearly to the top in mud.

Once inside the establishment, Felicity was relieved to discover the wooden planking scrubbed and glowing from a recent whitewash, and silently lamented the fact that she must track water and mud over the clean floor. The hall was filled with the savoury smell of cooking meat, and a large matron in a spotless apron looked at her with sympathy from an opposite doorway.

"Good gracious, mum, ye look fagged to death, if ye'll pardon me sayin' so. Ye'll be wantin' a room, I de'say. Priss will show ye up the stairs and git ye some hot water. Dinner's almost ready."

"Thank you," said Felicity, smiling her gratitude. "But first, tell me if a Lieutenant Kennedy and . . . and a young woman are staying here for the night? The lieutenant is a very tall Scottish gentleman with dark hair and brown eyes. The young woman is of medium height, very delicate, with auburn hair and hazel eyes."

"There's a tall man in the inn, but not by that name, mum," answered the matron, curiosity lighting her eyes. "And he's by hisself."

Felicity hid her disappointment under the guise of a smile. "My sister and her . . . husband were travelling this way," Felicity explained, feeling all the awkwardness of telling an untruth. "I hoped I might catch up with them." Then, having observed that the woman's dialect was different from that which she was used to hearing in Yorkshire, Felicity asked, "What is the name of your establishment and where is it located, if you please?"

"'Tis The Bull and Crown, Miss, in Kirkoswald, Cumbria,'' replied the innkeeper with considerable pride. Felicity was relieved to know they were still some distance from Gretna Green. Her sister must have also been delayed by the storm and stopped somewhere for the night. She fervently hoped Lieutenant Kennedy had been gentlemanly enough to procure them separate rooms.

"When my coachman comes in from the stables, please see that he is given a warm room and a warm meal as well,'' she requested of the woman. "Is your parlour occupied? I should like to have my dinner in there, if it's convenient.''

The innkeeper and his wife exchanged puzzled looks, and Felicity perceived that the innkeeper was still standing at the door, which he held slightly ajar. After peering one last time into the courtyard, he enquired in wondering accents, "Ye're alone then, mum?''

"Quite,'' Felicity replied lightly. "Except, of course, for Hugo, my coachman. I'll be dining alone!''

"Not if you intend to eat your dinner in the parlour,'' came a low masculine drawl from behind her. Felicity spun round and was startled to discover herself face to waistcoat with a gentleman. This was an unusual circumstance for Felicity and she could only think of one man tall enough to allow for such a thing to happen—Kyle Kennedy, her sister's would-be groom. But she heard no trace of Lieutenant Kennedy's Scottish lilt in this gentleman's deep voice.

"I've bespoke the parlour for my own use," the gentleman continued, "but am willing to share it, if you've no objection to the company."

Felicity lifted her eyes from the silver grey waist-coat, past a white cravat tied with elegant simplicity, to the finely chiseled features of one of the hand-somest men she'd ever clapped eyes on. Strangely enough, with his height, his rather longish raven hair and brilliant black eyes, he seemed almost an older, darker version of Lieutenant Kennedy.

Despite the daunting effect of such a vulcan god, Felicity knew she must waste no time in putting him properly in his place.

"I do not know you, sir," she informed him frostily and with a quelling look. "Therefore I've no intention of sharing my dinner with you."

The vulcan god grinned, his dancing black brows lending even more expression to the sparkling depths of his eyes. "It seems we are related through mar-riage."

"How is that possible? We've never met before!" Felicity returned scornfully, thinking him the out-side of enough. Did he think her a fool?

"The parlour door was open. I heard you asking about Lieutenant Kennedy and his, er, wife, who I gather is your sister?"

Felicity nodded, miserably aware she'd run into an unfortunate complication. "You are related to the lieutenant?'' she asked in the tone of one dreading the answer.

"Yes. He is my cousin,'' answered the vulcan god. "His father and my mother were brother and sister,'' he further explained.

The physical resemblance between them striking her now rather forcefully, Felicity had half-expected him to say he was the lieutenant's brother. But even as Lieutenant Kennedy's cousin, this imposing stranger presented a problem. Trying hard to subdue the stab of alarm twisting through her, Felicity fell into a fit of the babbles.

"Oh, you misunderstood,'' she said, laughing affectedly. "Who did you think I said, pray tell? Kennedy? But my sister is married to a Lieutenant *Cranley!* We are to meet in Maryport for a funeral, you see, my aunt Nancy having succumbed at last to the consumption—poor dear! And I only thought that I might have caught up with them along the way, what with this dreadful storm and all—''

"Cut line, my dear,'' the gentleman interrupted her, a maddeningly tolerant, amused smile curving his lips. "I don't know you, but you don't strike me as a gabble-grinder!''

Felicity was silenced.

"However, I congratulate you on your resourcefulness under fire, but it is a waste of time. I clearly heard you say my cousin's name and describe him quite accurately. Since I am well aware that Kyle has only recently returned from a campaign in France, you can imagine my surprise to learn of his marriage! Since there hasn't been time enough to publish the banns, they must have been wed by special licence! My cup of curiosity runneth over, Miss, er..." He raised those devilish brows.

"Felicity Bell," she answered mechanically, a knot tightening in her stomach.

"Miss Felicity Bell!" He said her name with relish, seeming to test the sound of it on his tongue. "Miss Bell, if you would be so good as to join me in the parlour after you've, er—" he cast keen, discerning eyes over her wrinkled dress and muddied boots "—tidied up, we can gossip about our mutual relatives over dinner." He turned to go, then turned back. "How rude of me! I did not introduce myself, did I? Jamieson Denham, Earl of Hastings at your service, Miss Bell! Now run along, won't you? I'm ravenous!"

Then, without waiting for her reply, Lord Hastings turned to enter a room Felicity supposed to be the parlour, taking care to duck his head in order to pass through the low door without blacking his eye.

Felicity stared after his retreating back with a jumble of emotions. What an arrogant man! The way he seemed to expect her to obey his command willy-nilly was the outside of enough! Felicity was not used to being told what to do!

"Will ye come with me, mum?" A maid Felicity assumed was Priss was standing on the stairs. Suddenly aware that the innkeeper and his wife, as well as the maid, had been privy to her conversation with Lord Hastings, Felicity was mortified. Never the less, she schooled her face into an expression of cool unconcern and followed the girl upstairs to her room.

The small bedchamber was clean and comfortable. Felicity hastily washed up, changed into the robin's-egg blue dress Chloe had packed for her, recombed her hair into a loose knot of curls at the crown of her head and descended the stairs. She paused at the parlour door. She wondered how the earl would react to the news of his cousin's elopement. Would he think her mad for pursuing them? She frowned. But why shouldn't she be concerned about her sister?

Then another thought occurred to her causing her pulse to race. The earl could very probably supply her with information about the lieutenant that would either set her mind at ease or confirm her worst fears. An urgency surged through her and she reached for the doorknob.

Lord Hastings was standing by the fire when she walked into the room. He did not look up as she approached as he was rather involved in briskly buffing an apple with his napkin. The table had been set for dinner and pushed cozily near the fire. She stopped just opposite the earl and watched as he finished his task and took a bite.

"Would you like one?" he offered, gesturing towards a bowl of fruit on a side table. "I couldn't wait for dinner."

"No, thank you," Felicity said. "I'm not very hungry tonight."

"Well, I'm always hungry," confessed the earl with a smile. "Comes of keeping this huge body of mine supplied with sufficient nourishment!"

Felicity could well imagine that this was true. His tall, muscular figure was imposing. But she'd wager there wasn't an ounce of fat on him! She blushed at her untoward thoughts and wrenched her eyes from his tight-fitting pantaloons.

"I can eat even when I'm worried, Miss Bell. But I suspect that some sort of worry accounts for your own lack of appetite tonight. Am I right?" Lord Hastings took another bite.

"Shall we dispense with guessing games, Lord Hastings, and get to the crux of the matter?" Felicity was appalled by the slightly waspish tone of her voice. But she was impatient to tell and hear the worst, and get it over with quickly. How could he stand there eating an apple so calmly?

"All right, then," said the earl, crossing his arms over his chest and fixing her with his complete, sober attention. "Explain your reasons for travelling unaccompanied through the wilderness of Cumbria in search of my cousin and your sister. Have they eloped?"

Felicity fell into a chair, laughing softly. "You're no chuckle-head, my lord!" she admitted.

"Thank you!" he replied emphatically. "Given the facts, it was a simple enough deduction to make.

But why are you following them? Unaccompanied, I might again add! Are you against the union?''

"Not really," hedged Felicity. Did she dare admit to the earl that she wanted to be sure the lieutenant wasn't a fortune-hunter? Lord Hastings waited for her answer, methodically devouring his apple while he rocked back and forth gently on the heels of his boots.

"Susan hardly knows your cousin, Lord Hastings, and we know nothing of him!"

"We?" prompted the earl.

"Henry—my brother—and I. Since our father died four years ago, Susan has lived with Henry. She is only seventeen and Henry stands as her guardian."

"I see. Go on."

"Well, your cousin spoke little of himself, saying only that he was of the Clan Kennedy from the coast of Carrick in southern Scotland."

"He was no doubt too involved in the agreeable task of wooing your sister to be much inclined for conversation," opined the earl, leaning back to rest his shoulders against the mantelpiece.

"While Henry and I found him to be a likable fellow, none of our friends could tell us anything about the Kennedys. And since Susan inherits a considerable amount of money, and given the rapidity of his attachment to her, we were afraid he might be a . . . well, a . . ." Felicity hardly knew how to say it without seeming rude.

Lord Hastings finished his apple and threw the core into the fireplace. "A fortune-hunter? Don't worry. I shan't be offended. Your concern is perfectly understandable. Now, let me put your mind at ease by telling you this. Kyle will be one of the richest men in Scotland. He is heir to Grandfather's titles, the most distinguished of them being Marquess of Ailsa. Grandfather is also Chieftain of the Clan Kennedy, another sort of title Kyle will inherit and one which carries considerable honour in Scotland. Grandfather's principal seat includes several hundred acres of wooded shore and a huge edifice on the coast of Carrick called Castle Culzean. Plump in the pocket is an understatement in the case of Lord Ailsa's fortune. I wonder Kyle did not mention these considerable assets as an inducement for your approval?"

Felicity was happy to hear that the lieutenant wasn't penniless, but she had never expected or required him to be as rich as a nabob, either. Now she was much easier in her mind about the lieutenant's intentions towards Susan. But something about Lord Hastings's matter-of-fact recital of his cousin's future wealth, and that last question, made her feel defensive.

"I'm relieved to hear he's not after her money, my lord," she returned with a toss of her head. "But pray tell, I hope you do not think I would have thrown my sister, or *myself,* at the fellow just because he is wealthy! Titles and wealth do not make the man, you know. I only wanted to be sure he truly loved her!''

Lord Hastings's brows lifted in appreciative surprise, and his black eyes widened and sparkled in the firelight. "I had not meant to give the impression that I thought of you, or your sister, as that sort of a female, Miss Bell. And I laud your sentiments. So many women of my acquaintance find wealth and titles the only qualities necessary in a prospective groom.''

Felicity was half inclined to be angry at the earl's slighting remark towards the female sex. But, in truth, she knew women like that, as well. And now the spell of his Gypsy eyes and the half-mocking, half-tender curve of his lips nipped her rising ire in the bud.

"Kyle is so used to his easy position, and so well known in his corner of Great Britain, that it probably never occurred to him that his motives or background might be questioned,'' the earl presently observed, leaning back against the mantelpiece again.

"Unfortunately one learns to be a trifle cynical,'' Felicity said, sighing. "It does not do to be too trusting. And Susan is so young!''

The earl smiled mockingly and gazed at Felicity through hooded eyes. "Would that she had the wisdom of your much advanced years, Miss Bell. But even with so many experiences behind you, you are too trusting, as well. Whatever possessed you to take to the road without so much as an abigail to lend you countenance?''

''Henry was not at hand to pursue the eloping couple,'' Felicity returned rigidly. ''And since my companion and my abigail were both bedridden with colds, I came alone. As you must acknowledge, a spinster of some five-and-twenty years need not guard her reputation as zealously as a young girl on the look-out for a husband.''

''What about your safety?'' he demanded, leaning slightly forward. ''There are men to be encountered everywhere who will not care a jot whether you are a spinster! They will see you only as a dammed attractive female!''

''Oh, do not be absurd, Lord Hastings,'' admonished Felicity, forcing a light laugh. In truth she was flustered by his compliment. ''You begin to sound like Henry, or Wenthorp, Susan's betrothed who was hand-picked by Henry!''

Lord Hastings straightened up. ''Your sister is betrothed to someone?''

''Yes. But never fear. Your cousin isn't in any immediate danger from the wrath of a jilted lover. Wenthorp doesn't know about the elopement as yet. And even when he does find out, I don't think he'll do anything about it. He's much too civilized.''

''Thank God!'' muttered the earl. ''It would hardly be fitting or fair for Kyle to receive a ball in his chest *after* he'd survived the war!''

"Henry likes Wenthorp very well," Felicity continued musingly. "But *he* is not required to marry the prosy fellow, though I doubt not they'd get on swimmingly together! I suppose elopement seemed the easiest, quickest way for Susan and the lieutenant to be together." Then, almost to herself, "I only hope she is truly in love with the lieutenant and didn't run off with him just to escape Wenthorp or Henry."

Felicity fell into a brown study and the earl remained silent. Presently there was a knock at the door. Felicity assumed that dinner was finally ready, but when Lord Hastings called "Enter!" it wasn't Priss or the innkeeper's wife to enter the room with covered dishes; it was Hugo.

"What is it, Hugo?" asked Felicity, rising to her feet.

"'Tis the carriage, miss," he answered, his hat respectfully clasped to his chest, his damp hair plastered to his ruddy scalp. "Three spokes in the left rear wheel is busted. There's no way we can leave at cock's crow, miss. The innkeeper's coaches are all hired out. All he's got is a gig and you can't go t' Scotland in a gig, miss. There's nothing for it, but t'get a wheelwright first thing in the morning."

"Oh, no, Hugo!" Felicity exclaimed. "That cannot be! Susan and Lieutenant Kennedy will be married by the time we can acquire the services of a wheelwright! No doubt they have been delayed by the storm, just as we have, but they will outdistance us tomorrow easily if we must stop for repairs!"

Hugo shrugged helplessly. Felicity turned to Lord Hastings. "Oh, dear, now what's to do?" she said, suppressing an urge to wring her hands in the dramatic fashion of Sarah Siddons.

"You must turn round and go back home," the earl replied practically. "I can't help but feel your errand rather unnecessary, and in the light of your lack of escort, unnecessarily dangerous. Susan is quite safe with Kyle. Leave her to make her own decisions!"

"But don't you understand? While you have quite set my mind at ease on the question of Lieutenant Kennedy's intentions towards Susan, I still must know for myself if she has thought this through! That is, if she truly wishes to marry him, or is just escaping the prospect of marriage to Wenthorp, or scoldings from Henry, or even another Season!" Felicity began to pace the floor, but was suddenly struck with an inspiring thought. "I know!" she cried, spinning round to face the earl. "You can drive me!"

Lord Hastings looked as though he didn't know whether to laugh or indulge in a fit of anger. Clearly he was astounded. "Good God, woman! Have you lost your mind? Besides, I've just come from Scotland and have business to attend to in Devon!"

"Please, Lord Hastings," implored Felicity, moving to stand directly in front of him. "I'll pay you! Please take me to Gretna Green!"

CHAPTER TWO

LORD HASTINGS STARED DOWN into eyes that were as green as the meadows of the Isle of Arran in spring. Wisps of flaming red hair framed a flushed, oval face. The rosebud lips were parted expectantly as she waited for his answer. God, but she was a beauty! How was it possible that she'd never wed?

"As I said before, Miss Bell," he hedged, stepping back and away from the light scent of roses which hung about her, "I've just come from Scotland. In fact, I was visiting Grandfather at Culzean when Kyle sent word of his safe arrival in London. I left the old fellow in the midst of plans to welcome his grandson home from the war."

"That's no excuse!" declared Miss Bell with a toss of her fiery curls. "This is a case of urgency, and besides, I fully expect we will catch them up before they've even reached the border at Gretna Green! Then you may go on your merry way home to England! By then Hugo will have had the carriage fixed and will have followed us to collect me."

"I hardly think it a case of urgency, Miss Bell. Besides, you are travelling alone," Lord Hastings reminded her, retreating round the table while she advanced. "If word were to surface that I dashed about Cumbria with an unattended female—that female being you!—your brother Henry would seek me out and I would find myself as close to parson's mousetrap as Cousin Kyle!"

"Not if I refused to marry you," scoffed Miss Bell. "Which I would! Besides, we will not be found out, I assure you!"

"You are a determined, managing sort of female, aren't you?" grumbled the earl. He was beginning to understand why Miss Bell hadn't married.

"If you won't take me I shall go in a gig to the next coaching house and hire a carriage from there! That is, if one is available. I am determined to follow her!"

Lord Hastings was faced with a dilemma. The idea of this carrot-curled beauty travelling to the border in an open gig was appalling. Anyone—the lowest of creatures—might see her and take advantage of her defencelessness. And there was this wretched weather! Even if she wasn't ravished and robbed, the foolish girl might take cold and die of a fever! No, there seemed to be no way out of it. He was compelled to save Miss Bell from her own wilfulness.

His business in Devon might wait. She'd waited this long . . .

However, Miss Bell must understand that there would be certain rules. After all, if he didn't exercise some control over Miss Bell from the beginning, he'd no doubt she'd run roughshod over him in a pig's whisper.

"Miss Bell!" Lord Hastings had meant to sound forceful and commanding and was gratified to see the slight tremor ripple through Miss Bell. He stepped forward and she stepped back.

"I will escort you in this ill-advised pursuit of your sister because I am averse to reading about your untimely demise in the *Gazette!*" He took another step and she took two steps back, her eyes wide and unblinking. "But never—do you hear me? *Never* offer me money again! No, not even a halfpenny! Do you understand?"

"Yes," she answered softly, but promptly.

"And," he added, "if you should cause me the least inconvenience on this trip, if you prove to be too wilful to tolerate, I shall leave you at whatever dwelling we should happen to be passing at the time, where you may summon your coachman to fetch you at your leisure! Then you may be sure of never catching up with your sister!"

Hugo harrumphed indignantly, then coughed in an attempt to hide the disrespectful noise. He was obviously affronted by Lord Hastings's treatment of his beloved mistress. Miss Bell was probably just as offended, but she gave her coachman a gentle, admonishing look and turned back to the earl.

"Agreed!" she said at last. "But since I plan to have as little to do with you as possible, I can't see how I could cause you any inconvenience at all!"

Then she turned her back and exited the room in a flurry of blue muslin, nearly running into Priss on the threshold.

Vastly enjoying his leverage over Miss Bell, whom he was sure was not used to obliging anyone but herself, Lord Hastings called out in his most congenial voice, "Aren't you staying to take dinner with me?"

"I shall eat in my room!" was the uncongenial retort.

Lord Hastings chuckled. What had he got himself into?

SITTING ON THE EDGE of the bed, Lord Hastings shoved his stockinged foot into the sturdy Blucher boot his kneeling manservant, Jenson, held steady. This task completed, they rose in unison. Jenson then poised his lordship's rich claret coat in a position most conducive to easing muscular arms and a broad back into precisely cut shoulder seams, and Lord Hastings shrugged into it. Since his lordship had already arranged his neckcloth *en cascade,* ruining only three in the process, all Jenson had left to do was hand him the various accoutrements which would provide the finishing touches: a silver fob watch, signet ring, gilded *tabatière* and alabaster handkerchief.

"Do you think the young lady will be ready to go, sir?" asked Jenson with studied indifference.

"I hope so," replied the earl. "An early start is essential since the weather shows no signs of cooperating today. The roads will be ghastly!'' He walked over to the window and frowned down on the muddy front courtyard of The Bull and Crown. It was a grey, mizzling morning. The sun had made a dismal debut, its faded face showing vaguely through the cloud cover like an aged woman through a veil.

"Perhaps I should send a maid to her door, my lord," said Hugo, her coachman. "Being that she has no abigail or companion, she may still be abed."

"Yes, perhaps you should send a maid," agreed the earl, his frown increasing. "Dash it, how I wish the woman *did* have an abigail or someone along! I'm quite sure I shall find it deucedly uncomfortable travelling with her alone! But the fool girl might have come to a dreadful end in some ditch had I not agreed to drive her in my carriage!"

Jenson nodded his head soberly. "Yes, my lord. Mr. Hugo had said as much to me himself, quite understanding your reasons for escorting his mistress, but has beseeched me to, er, guard Miss Bell's, er, virtue!"

Lord Hastings grinned humourlessly. "Oh, did he? How quaint. Even though I stand as her protector, he thinks I might find myself unable to resist temptation, does he? He needn't worry! Unless the fellow attempting the ravishing were a complete brute, willing to beat her senseless for the pleasure of it, I passionately believe Miss Bell capable of guarding her own virtue! Hugo may rest assured that I need not go to such lengths to embrace a comely

woman's charms. Now go and have the virtuous
damsel rousted out of her bed, if you please! We've
a coach and four to catch up with and no time to
lose. I'll be having my breakfast.''

With these orders Lord Hastings left the room,
deftly dipping his head beneath the doorframe and
briskly descending the narrow inn stairs two at a
time. On the way to the parlour, he grabbed an apple out of a bowl sitting on a table in the entry-hall,
and commenced polishing it with his fresh handkerchief. When he entered the parlour, he was startled
to discover Miss Bell just rising from the table. After a cursory inspection of the plate in front of her,
sprinkled with breadcrumbs and with a knife neatly
laid over top of it, he was mortified to conclude she
had been up and about long before himself.

''Here you are at last,'' she greeted him graciously, her smile oozing wicked delight. ''I had begun to think you would sleep away the morning. I
know how you fashionable gentlemen are!''

Lord Hastings's eyes flickered over her. She
looked as fresh as a hawthorn flower in that rose-
coloured dress, though her titian hair gave her more
the appearance of an exotic bloom. Did orchids
come in just that shade, he wondered? Then, gathering his wits, he glanced at the mantel clock and
coolly replied, ''Tis only six o'clock, Miss Bell. I
thought it would be useless to rise any earlier, knowing how you fashionable ladies are!''

"Ah, but I am determined not to inconvenience you, Lord Hastings," she purred, batting a pair of ridiculously long lashes. "I hope you will at least try to return the favour!"

"Oh, of course, Miss Bell," he replied with a congenial smile as he seated his long frame in the reed-backed chair by the table. "I intend to give back all that I get!"

It was apparent to Lord Hastings from Miss Bell's raising of one brow and withering look, that she had understood his meaning. At least he was not doomed to spend several hours in a closed carriage with a henwit.

"I will see to my bag, Lord Hastings, and leave instructions for Hugo to meet me in Gretna," she finally said with a haughty lift of her chin. "Pray, do not keep me waiting overly long whilst you polish the apples!"

Lord Hastings kept his face perfectly impassive until Miss Bell left the room, then he smiled and took a large bite of his shining apple. Miss Bell was obviously at a disadvantage, what with having to depend entirely upon him for transportation, but she wasn't about to grovel. He decided it was refreshing to spar with a spirited woman. Most respectable women of his acquaintance were not nearly so entertaining.

While the maidservant placed several dishes in front of him, Lord Hastings contemplated his cousin's marriage to Susan Bell. No doubt it would come as a surprise to their grandfather that Kyle had not chosen a Scottish lass to wed. As Chieftain of the Clan Kennedy, it would be essential that Kyle took to wife a woman willing to embrace the Scottish traditions so important to the clansmen. Was Susan Bell such a woman?

While Lord Ailsa had no strong aversion to the English, still he had lived through the turmoil surrounding the Battle of Culloden, the last Jacobite uprising led by Bonnie Prince Charlie. Their great-grandfather, a staunch Jacobite wishing to see Scotland independent from England, had fallen in that battle. Only a lad, yet still chieftain by patriarchal order, Lord Ailsa had held the clan together through the suppression which followed, when no Scot was allowed to wear the kilt, bear arms or play the bagpipe.

When the suppression was lifted in '82, Lord Ailsa led the celebrations with a gathering of the clan, where the playing of bagpipes by enthusiastic pipers (who were sadly out of practice) frightened the horses and sent a flock of sheep stampeding. But no matter—to Lord Ailsa it was the sweetest music ever!

However, despite his devotion to Scotland and the ways of the clan, Lord Ailsa was no fool. He saw the great good sense of Scotland's union with Britain. But while he mixed with the English at social gatherings during his infrequent visits to Edinburgh, Lord Ailsa had never journeyed to London. Thus, it was no wonder Miss Bell's friends could not enlighten her on the circumstances of the Kennedy family of Carrick.

Lord Hastings was much like his grandfather in this respect. He attended social functions in Town, but no more than were necessary to observe standard politeness. And though he was born and raised in Devon, he was as much Scottish as English. In fact, he felt himself a comfortable blend of both his Scottish mother and his English father, neither of whom had been much enamoured of the social whirl of London. After once or twice plunging himself headlong into the pleasures and pitfalls of a London Season, Lord Hastings knew he much preferred the quiet stateliness of his principal seat in Devon, or the serene grandeur of the Scottish countryside.

As for the diversion of a ladybird, Lord Hastings had always installed mistresses in houses in nearby towns, such as Exeter. He never deemed it really practical to post to London every time he had an amorous urge! If truth be told, having a mistress at all was becoming rather wearisome. They tended to sulk when he left them alone for too long. Even now he had to return to England to give Kate, a buxom blond beauty, her congé, though he had much rather stay at Culzean.

Lord Hastings loved Culzean, a fondness grown from his frequent holidays there as a youth. Indeed, he and Kyle had been so much together that they were more brothers than cousins. He had been terribly relieved to learn of Kyle's safe return from France.

It hadn't been necessary for Kyle to join the Highlander troops in defence of Great Britain against the monster, Napoleon. Since his father had been killed in a hunting accident years before, Kyle was next in line to inherit Culzean. He certainly did not need an army career. But Kyle was a passionate, impulsive young man, and he had joined the corps, anyway. Indeed, Lord Hastings had been strongly tempted to join the Royal Dragoons himself. But with his father's protracted illness and finally his death, Lord Hastings had been needed at home.

But where was his mind wandering? He had been pondering the idea of Kyle's English bride-to-be. While their grandfather would not shun her because she wasn't Scottish but English, she would have to work harder to gain acceptance. Indeed, he again hoped she was a spirited lass, just like her sister.

Her sister. Yes, it was admirable the way Miss Bell was determined to ensure her sister's happiness. But Susan had made a decision and ought to be left to herself. No doubt Miss Bell was well-meaning, but her concern bordered on the meddlesome in Lord Hastings's opinion. But he couldn't leave the headstrong baggage to her own devices, that was certain. A gig, indeed!

"Would ye like coffee, sir, or tea?"

Lord Hastings blinked once or twice and turned his eyes to the maid standing by the table. "Coffee, please," he replied.

The maid poured the coffee, and Lord Hastings drank the scalding liquid in a gulp, immediately requesting more. He was quite sure he'd need plenty of fortification for the day ahead.

LORD HASTINGS'S ENQUIRIES at the various inns along the Cumbric Road revealed the runaway couple were about an hour ahead. And no matter how much the horses were urged through the peaty slough, they were never able to narrow that measure of time between them. They'd left Carlisle behind some two hours ago, and by the calculations in her guidebook, Felicity felt sure that Gretna Green must be just over the next rise.

"I wish I'd eaten something in Carlisle!" grumbled Lord Hastings, who sat next to Felicity in the coach so they could both face forward and watch for their troublesome relatives. Jenson sat across from them, saying nothing but eyeing them with the unrelenting scrutiny of a chaperon, which would have pleased Hugo very much.

"How can you think of food now!" exclaimed Felicity. "I couldn't eat a morsel!"

"Yes, but you've been conserving your energy, Miss Bell," the earl replied pointedly. "You slept from Kirkoswald to Warwick."

"I was tired! I was up half the night, if you must know!" she snapped back. She was a little defensive about falling asleep for the greater part of the trip, especially since she'd awakened to find her face pressed against the earl's shoulder, her bonnet askew and falling down the back of her head. She must have been a sight!

"And you were up much earlier than your usual time, no doubt," Lord Hastings further observed, his black eyes daring her to deny it.

Felicity did not reply. She would not give him the satisfaction. Obviously, Lord Hastings became quarrelsome when he was hungry, which was most of the time. Instead, she made a show of being completely engrossed in her travel guide.

"By Jupiter, there's the River Esk at last!" his lordship presently shouted. "Just over the bridge will be Gretna! Thank God, I thought we'd never get here!"

Felicity looked through the window and saw they were approaching a wide stretch of river spanned by a stone bridge. Just ahead were a few nondescript cottages clustered about a small grove of firs. For a town of such notoriety, Gretna Green certainly did not appear out of the ordinary. And in the opaque grey of a drizzly afternoon, it looked downright dreary.

They crossed the bridge and pulled up to the only public establishment the village seemed to boast. It was called The Anvil. Felicity wondered if this was an enterprising innkeeper's idea of humour, since couples fleeing to Gretna Green were said to be married "over the anvil," an expression derived from the ability of any Scottish citizen, from fisherman to blacksmith, to unite them in holy matrimony.

Since no ostler rushed out to lead the horses to the stable and no one appeared at the door, Lord Hastings disembarked and assisted Felicity from the carriage. After a quick assessment of the courtyard, which held no clue of the couple's whereabouts since there wasn't a carriage in sight, they entered the inn.

Felicity shook the wrinkles out of her skirt, anxiously scanning the empty entry-hall while Lord Hastings paced. Since she felt sure he was not in the least interested in whether Kyle and Susan married, she attributed Lord Hastings's impatience to hunger and a desire to be rid of her company, which had been thrust upon him quite against his will.

"Where is everybody?" he growled. He flung open two or three doors leading off the main hall and peered inside each one. Felicity saw that one of them was a parlour. It was empty but the fire was lit and a table was set for dining. The appearance of plateware must have reminded the earl of his hunger because he seemed to grow more impatient than ever. His black eyes sparked life like flint onyx as they raked the hall for signs of life. Then, spying a handbell resting on a small table, he walked over to it and shook the bell violently. The resulting din could not fail to be heard in every corner of the house.

Soon a door opened at the far end of the narrow hall and an elderly woman in a dark woollen dress and green-and-red tartan smock approached them. "Goodness, dinna ye have any respect for the institution of marriage?" she scolded, wagging a gnarled finger reproachfully. "There's a weddin' goin' on!"

"Good heavens!" exclaimed Felicity, grasping the earl's forearm. "It must be Susan and Kyle, my lord! Stop them! *Do* stop them, so I can talk to her first! Please, Lord Hastings!"

"Good God!" grumbled the earl, but he moved quickly forward and down the hall.

Felicity scampered after him, as well as the woman, who had no doubt understood his lordship's intent, and was wildly flinging her arms in the air, shouting, "Duncan! Duncan! Here's another one come to make trouble!"

His black eyes flashing, Lord Hastings burst through the door and into the room the woman had so recently vacated. There was a scream, a heavy thud and then a string of curses. Felicity entered the room to discover Lord Hastings held at pistol-point by the self-appointed minister, who was most probably the innkeeper, a thin, callow-looking gentleman prostrate on the floor, and a white-faced chit clutching her breast. No doubt standing as witnesses, two servants cowered in the background.

"Ye're too late, lad!" declared the innkeeper, jauntily wagging the gun in front of Lord Hastings's face. "They're shackled right and proper! The rings ha' been exchanged and there's nothing ye kin do about it! Now go about yer business and dinna make a scene or I'll have ta take measures agin ye!''

If Lord Hastings was embarrassed by their mistake, or intimidated by the pistol aimed at a point between his eyes, it wasn't apparent by his expression. In fact, one would suppose the innkeeper had been the one to err.

"Put that pistol away," his lordship muttered disgustedly. "I've no objection to this particular marriage! And sit that girl down! She's about to swoon. And madam . . ." He turned to face the innkeeper's wife. "Have you some whiskey to administer to the poor fellow on the floor?" The woman nodded. "Good! Once you've restored the couple to their senses I've some questions for you. We shall await you in the parlour and when you join us do *not* fail to bring food. My, er, *sister* and I are sharp set after our travels." Lord Hastings turned on his heel, grasped Felicity by the elbow and propelled her to the door.

Turning abruptly at the threshold he said, "Oh, I almost forgot. I beg your pardon for my blunder, madam." He sketched the pale bride an elegant bow. "And convey my sincere apologies to your husband, as well!" The inhabitants of the room, except, of course, for the still insensible bridegroom, were left staring mutely, their mouths agape.

Shuttled pell-mell down the hall, Felicity expelled a lungful of breath she'd been holding and stared up at her escort with awe. "You're a cool one, aren't you? Weren't you afraid that man was going to kill you?"

"Why should he? I merely made a mistake," was his unflappable reply.

"Rather it was *I* who made the mistake, my lord," confessed Felicity. "You would not have gone in there had I not begged you to do so!" She paused. "But the look in your eyes when you burst through the door... It seemed almost as if you wished to stop the marriage, as well. Is that possible?" Felicity searched his face.

Suddenly Lord Hastings stopped dragging Felicity down the hall like a recalcitrant child and fixed those black eyes upon her. "Perhaps I do feel some concern over the suitability of the match," he admitted.

"Tell me why!" insisted Felicity.

"I shall, after we eat!"

And Felicity found she had to be satisfied to wait. Standing thus in the narrow hallway, staring back at the earl, Felicity's mind wandered away from Susan's predicament and fell to speculating on other, more intriguing thoughts.

Besides the ravenous hunger that seemed to possess him from time to time, Felicity sensed a passion and intensity boiling beneath the surface of this English nobleman that was barely held in check by his outward elegance. The way he'd burst into the wedding chamber seemed a perfect example of this hidden passion! Then, unbidden to her virgin's mind, came the thought, *Does he bring that same passion and intensity to his lovemaking?*

Felicity felt herself trembling, whether from fear or something a little more sinful, she wasn't sure. Suddenly her immersion in the earl's black eyes was interrupted when he fairly shouted, "Zounds, my girl! Why do you look at me in such a way, and why do you tremble? I shan't eat you!" he reassured her, the dangerous glint in his eyes joined by amusement. "Though if I'm not fed soon, I may be tempted to do so! Starting here!" He drew one of her earlobes between his thumb and forefinger and pulled on it with sensuous deliberation.

Knowing full well she ought to slap him, Felicity was too overwhelmed by strange sensations to do anything. Thank God, Jenson chose that moment to enter the inn. The manservant's eyes were riveted to Lord Hastings's hand as he removed it from her earlobe, but Jenson's face remained impassive.

"My lord," he said, "once I rousted the sleeping ostler and made some enquiries, I could discover no trace of your cousin having been here. Though it *was* rather difficult to communicate with the fellow since he was, er, in his cups, so to speak. He said he'd only watered and fed horses for two couples today and neither description matches that of Lieutenant Kennedy and Miss Bell. And your cousin, with his prodigious height, is not easily missed."

The earl grimaced. "Drat! I was sure we'd catch them up before the ceremony, or at least before they'd retired to the Nuptial Room! But it appears they had no intention of stopping at Gretna at all!" At Felicity's puzzled look, he explained. "The Nuptial Room is an apartment supplied by an establishment on an hourly basis, Miss Bell, so that if the wedding couple wishes to consummate the marriage and be on their way, they need not incur the expense for an entire night's lodging."

Felicity blushed. "Do not take me for an addlepate! I know what a Nuptial Room is, Lord Hastings!" she lied. "If I appear nonplussed it's because I don't understand your reasoning. Susan would not have run off with your cousin if she did not intend to marry him! She wrote in her note that they were going to Gretna Green to be married!"

Lord Hastings shrugged. "Doubtless they were headed this way, but it does not appear that they stopped to be married!"

Felicity was getting angry. Did he suppose her sister a common strumpet?

So involved were the three in their discussion that they hadn't heard the innkeeper approaching. "If ye're lookin' for a long-shanks with a pretty young lassie with ginger hair, a mite more brownish than yours, miss, they stopped here, all right, but they dinna stay. I tended to the horses meself, since the ostler—the devil take'im!—could'na. The tall lad

bespoke a dish of tea for the lass and use of the con-
veniences, and then they was off.''

Felicity was incredulous. "They didn't ask to be
married?"

"Nay, miss," said the innkeeper, seemingly glad
to be of help now that he'd stored away his pistol.
"Said they was goin' up t' Castle Culzean." The
innkeeper grinned broadly. "I'm a Gordon meself,
but me'wife, she's from the Clan Kennedy. We was
that pleased t'hear they were goin' t' be married
proper-like by his grandfather, the chieftain hisself!"

Felicity turned questioning eyes to Lord Hastings, whose cautious look convinced her to keep silent. It was obvious the earl did not want to carry
forth a discussion in front of the innkeeper, so she
had to force herself to wait till they were alone to
bombard him with questions and conjectures.

The opportunity came when they were seated for
a light meal and the innkeeper's wife had supplied
them with food and left them alone. However, Felicity applied the good sense of allowing the earl
several bites to take the edge off his hunger before
she began.

This process took longer than she had thought,
because no matter how sharp set Lord Hastings had
professed himself to be, he did not wolf down his
food but rather ate it with savouring restraint. This
naturally gave rise to another intriguing surmise

about a possible similarity between Lord Hastings's personality and his lovemaking.

Firmly suppressing such untoward thoughts, Felicity finally asked, "Why do you suppose Kyle did not marry Susan at Gretna Green and..." The second half of her question was more difficult to express. "Do you really think he plans to marry her?"

"Of course he plans to marry her," Lord Hastings replied briefly, not the least offended by Felicity's doubts. "Kyle is an honourable man."

Felicity sighed with relief. "I believe you. And I begin to suspect that I've been overly concerned about this whole affair. If he's actually taking Susan up to present her to your grandfather, Kyle must truly love her."

"Knowing Kyle's impulsive, but completely devoted and loyal nature, I've no doubt he loves her," agreed the earl.

Felicity fell to pondering and shortly the earl said, "But you still want to hear, from her own lips, your sister's feelings for Kyle. Am I correct?"

"Yes. But not only that, I want to know why *you* have doubts about the suitability of the match."

Lord Hastings's brows drew together in a slight frown. He set down his knife and fork and looked musingly at the fire. "Grandfather is Scottish through and through. He would more readily welcome your sister as a granddaughter if she were Scottish. My father, who was an Englishman, had the devil of a time at first when he attempted to court

my mother. But once he had earned Grandfather's
respect, it became much easier for everyone. But now
that Kyle is to become chieftain of the clan, he will
require a wife who will suit him as such. Furthermore, if the clansmen do not take a fancy to your
sister, she may feel uncomfortable in such a role. If
Grandfather likes her, that is half the battle won.
However, Grandfather *can* be...a trifle...in-
timidating." He paused.

Felicity tried hard not to show her discomfiture.
Poor Susan! Poor timid, sensitive Susan!

"Do not look so crestfallen," advised the earl in
a bracing tone. "If Susan is anything like you, Miss
Bell, she will manage well enough." Though Felicity
kept her eyes fixed on her full plate, she could feel his
questioning gaze. "She *is* like you, isn't she?"

Felicity sighed. "Susan is as timid as a doe, easily
frightened, easily upset. When she's nervous she's as
clumsy as a newborn colt—all tangled legs! It takes
her a while to get used to people, but when she does,
she's all sweetness and warmth. Do you think your
grandfather will give Susan the time she needs to get
used to him?" Felicity looked hopefully at the earl.

"Good God, I haven't even got used to the old
tartar yet!" the earl said with a laugh. When Felicity did not join in his laughter, but rather looked all
the more worried, Lord Hastings sobered.

"She will have a hard time of it at the castle, won't
she?" said Felicity.

"Kyle will help her," the earl assured her in the tone of one trying to convince himself as well. "We... *You* must let them work this out for themselves, Miss Bell. Susan has chosen to spend her life with Kyle, and she must either do so, or cry off!"

"I ought to be with her," cried Felicity. "I ought at least to be with her for the wedding! She will have need of me! You do plan to take me to Castle Culzean, don't you, Lord Hastings?"

"I'm sure Hugo will have had your carriage repaired by now," the earl demurred in a strained voice. Didn't she see the unsuitability, nay, the danger, of their travelling together? "Didn't you leave orders with Hugo to follow us to Gretna Green at the first possible opportunity? Hugo can take you the rest of the way."

"That will take too much time! Whether they wed immediately or not, Susan will have need of me—I'm sure of it!"

Lord Hastings was no proof against Miss Bell's wide green-eyed plea for assistance. If truth be told, he had developed rather a strong interest in the outcome of the elopement, as well. To be sure, he cared very much that Kyle was happily wed and that his wife was accepted by Grandfather, if for no other reason than a desire for Kyle's comfort. And he did feel a measure of pity for Susan, and grudgingly admitted to himself that she would probably be made more comfortable by her sister's presence at the castle.

But it was more than that. Surely, if Miss Bell waited at Gretna for her carriage, the delay would not amount to much. But he found himself wishing to witness Miss Bell's descent on Castle Culzean and her meeting with Lord Ailsa firsthand. He had not been so vastly entertained in an age.

"I will take you to Culzean, Miss Bell," he consented with an exaggerated sigh.

She smiled gratefully, and he was so captivated by the brilliance of her expression that he was prompted to add, "But you will owe me something for agreeing to such a plan!"

"You said I was not to offer you another groat," she reminded him, surprised.

"I did not absolutely mention money as payment, now did I?" he teased.

Felicity stared at the earl, unbelieving, the heat rising in her cheeks. He was flirting with her! How dared he, when he knew she was virtually at his mercy while they travelled thus alone together!

The earl resumed eating and Felicity forced down a few bites of bread and cheese. She did not wish to inconvenience his lordship by fainting for lack of food. He might be obliged to lift her senseless body from the floor! She imagined his strong arms holding her and she could eat no more.

CHAPTER THREE

THEIR PROGRESS TOWARDS Castle Culzean was greatly hampered by the steady rain and an increasing gale from the North Channel. Despite the long twilights of Scotland, by eight o'clock it began to grow dark. Lord Hastings had frequently travelled this road and was on the lookout for The Ferry and Ferlie, a favourite inn of his which he occasionally patronized on the way to or from Culzean. When he saw the dim light of the inn glowing just ahead, he sighed with relief. He was eager for a good dinner and a dry, warm bed.

Wiping a clear patch in the foggy carriage window, he peered out over the familiar Scottish landscape. They were passing through a heavily wooded valley, with a boisterous creek running alongside the road, and he thought it a pity Miss Bell was not awake to enjoy the scenery. As they rounded a bend, he saw the large misty lake which was known locally as Loch Doon. Settled near its wooded shore was a white stucco building with dormer windows and steep roofs, The Ferry and Ferlie. It was a modern building, Georgian in design.

He glanced at Miss Bell. She couldn't seem to eat much of anything, but she was certainly having no trouble sleeping. He sighed. He knew she was anxious about her sister, but she was a game one, not easily discouraged!

He continued to observe his travelling companion. With her head rested against the other side of the carriage and her hands lying limply in her lap, the long slender fingers curled loosely round her guidebook, Miss Bell looked very tempting. Her rosy lips parted in sleep and her long lashes cast feathery shadows against her cheeks. His eyes slid farther down and he observed with a stirring appreciation the full curve of Miss Bell's bosom, the slim lines of her waist and the enticing swell of her hips. This was no schoolroom miss; this was a real woman!

Then, in the leisurely manner of a true connoisseur, he visually traversed her lush curves in an upward sweep until his eyes rested once again on her face. She was watching him. The accusing look in her eyes clearly stated that she recognized the lust in his.

''You're awake, Miss Bell!'' he exclaimed, trying to cover his naughty-boy-with-his-hand-caught-in-the-sugarbowl chagrin with a rallying tone. ''Just in time!'' Then he thumped thrice on the carriage ceiling with his cane, and George the coachman obeyed the signal to pull over.

The cobbled courtyard glistened slickly wet in the pool of light falling from a large lantern hanging from an awning over the front door. The sign could be clearly seen. Lord Hastings noticed Miss Bell's puzzled expression as she gazed at the sign and commented, "Yes, 'tis a strange name for an inn!" But he received no reply from Miss Bell. If he could judge by the set of her mouth and her sudden rapt contemplation of vacant air, she was not on speaking terms with him. "Perhaps over dinner I should tell you why it is named thusly. It is a fascinating tale, isn't it, *Jenson!*"

Jenson had been sleeping soundly, but Lord Hastings's sudden inclusion of his manservant into the conversation bestirred him sufficiently to mumble, "Just so, sir," not comprehending in the least as to what he was agreeing to.

Mr. Stuart, the innkeeper of The Ferry and Ferlie, was much more efficient at his duties than the man at The Anvil. This could be explained, however, by the fact that he generally was not troubled by eloping couples from England. And since he was well accustomed to enjoying Lord Hastings's frequent patronage, he ushered them into the entry-hall and out of the rain with solicitous haste.

Lord Hastings immediately made enquiries to ascertain if Kyle had stopped there. Since the inn had been quite busy that evening, the innkeeper could not say whether Kyle had stopped to change horses, but, of a certainty, he had not rented a room for the night.

"I hope you still have two rooms left, Mr. Stuart," said the earl, removing his curly beaver hat and spilling a rivulet of rain from its brim onto the spotless floor.

"I'm dreadful sorry, m'lord," apologized the innkeeper, stooping to wipe up the water with a clean cloth. "But yer men'll have to put up wit' the stablelads. I dinna have but one room left. Full up, I am." He eyed Miss Bell and came to his own conclusions, smiling broadly. "But yer lady'll like it well enough, m'lord. The bed is a mite small, but the sheets are clean!"

At this remark, Miss Bell, who had been hovering silently in the background, stepped forward and seemed ready to take the innkeeper to task for his mistaken idea. Lord Hastings lifted his hand in a silencing gesture. She glared at him, but closed her mouth and retreated a step.

"You misunderstand, Mr. Stuart," Lord Hastings explained patiently, greatly enjoying the affronted blush suffusing Miss Bell's lovely countenance. "This young woman is my sister, Miss Denham." Then he had a sudden mischievous inspiration. "Miss *Calamity* Denham!"

Mr. Stuart, as guileless as a child, regarded Miss Bell again quickly and said, "Aye. I see the family resemblance! Ye're both tall, ain't ye? But I still dinna have mor'an th'one room fit fer Quality, and if ye don't mind me sayin' so, m'lord, in these parts it ain't no matter if a brother and sister share their sleeping quarters. We kin put another cot in the room, m'lord!"

Lord Hastings considered this arrangement for a moment and said, "Yes, it will have to do. I've no mind to sleeping over the stables. It would be deucedly *inconvenient.* Don't you agree, Calamity, my dear?" he smoothly enquired, turning his head to watch Miss Bell's reaction to the innkeeper's countrified philosophy. "After all, we used to sleep together as children, didn't we?"

Miss Bell was staring at the floor, her bottom lip firmly clamped between her teeth. No doubt stubborn pride kept her from opposing the plan. She had promised not to cause him any inconvenience. Or perhaps she truly believed he'd carry out his threat to desert her if she caused him trouble. Lord Hastings subdued a chuckle. Thank God she thought him such a shameless rogue, or else he might have the devil of a time controlling her!

"Why don't you go on ahead with the maid, er, Calamity, and freshen up whilst I break the news to Jenson that he and George needs must sleep over the stable. You will have the room all to yourself. . . for now." Then he could not help himself. He conjured up the most lecherous look and devilish smile possible. He had the pleasure of observing her green eyes widen with alarm before she scooted after the maid up the stairs.

FELICITY SENT THE MAID to procure a screen behind which she might change her clothes. After observing the look in Lord Hastings's eyes in the coach and later in the hall of the inn, she would not put it past him to enter the room unannounced. The puzzled maid returned with only a blanket to hang from one nail to another in a corner of the small room, but Felicity was thankful for anything to help preserve her modesty.

Later, when she entered the parlour, she expected to find her tormentor warming his backside at the fire with a glass of good Scotch whiskey in his fist— or perhaps an apple—eager for his turn to wash up for dinner. She was disappointed when he wasn't there. He was probably loitering in the taproom, unless he'd gone upstairs directly from there. In either case it galled her no end to have to hold her spleen whilst he drank his fill or dallied over his toilette!

A half hour passed while she paced the floor in front of the fireplace. The disquieting thought came to her that his lordship *was* taking an inordinate amount of time to wash up for dinner. Then she remembered seeing two male servants carrying a copper tub up the narrow inn-stairs as she was coming down.

She stamped her foot! The bath must have been for *him!* How dared he bathe when she'd declined the luxury and hurried downstairs for fear of keeping the perpetually starving earl from his dinner! Then, worse still, she thought, *Good God, perhaps he is primping because he means to seduce me.*

With this possibility uppermost on her mind, it was no wonder that when Lord Hastings entered the parlour, fresh and spruce in elegant evening clothes, and smelling annoyingly clean, he was confronted by a raging termagant.

"If you think I'm going to share a room with you, Lord Hastings, you've gone completely noddy!" she informed him in wrathful accents, her glittering eyes raking over his imposing—and disturbing!—figure. "A more loggerheaded notion you couldn't possibly have conceived! And how dare you call me 'Calamity' in that odious way!"

"Be thankful that I refrained from calling you my wife, Miss Bell, since husbands and wives are frequently not averse to sleeping in the same room," he replied as he moved unhurriedly towards the heavy wooden mantel above the fireplace, which was lined with pottery, and leaned a shoulder against it. His eyes flickered over her. "Sometimes they even share the same bed." He paused while she squirmed. "I had the great good sense to introduce you as my sister in hopes of procuring you a separate bedchamber, or at least a separate bed."

"But must you have called me 'Calamity'?" she persisted, exasperated by the devil's unruffled calm.

"I did not suppose you wished your real name to be used in this instance. Calamity seemed a suitable substitute for Felicity. In fact, *more* suitable, in my opinion."

"No doubt you think me a perfect nuisance!" she hissed. "But—never fear!—I do not intend to cause you inconvenience by requesting that you sleep above the stables—"

"It shouldn't do you a smidgen of good even if you did ask me," he interrupted, pouring himself a glass of ale from a jug on the table.

"So I will take myself off after dinner and sleep in the carriage!" Having said her piece, and been gratified by the earl's stunned silence, Felicity sat down at the table and poured herself a tumbler of ale.

Lord Hastings recovered quickly. He said, "I shan't do that if I were you."

"And why not? It rains, but it is not very cold. As your carriage is extremely snug, I shall be protected sufficiently from drafts, and I shall take blankets with me, of course...."

"What will protect you from the 'beastie,' Miss Bell?" he asked suddenly, his eyes narrowing dangerously.

"What do you mean, my lord?" she quavered, unnerved by his strange expression.

"The loch beastie, Miss Bell."

"Stuff and nonsense!" she exclaimed, despite the chill down her spine.

"Let me tell you why the inn is named The Ferry and Ferlie. But first take a drink of your ale, my girl." He sat down opposite her and grinned.

Felicity bethought herself wise to follow the earl's advice and fortify herself with a swallow of ale. After two or three swallows she felt much braver. "I can't imagine what humbug you've contrived to frighten me, Lord Hastings, but I shall probably find the attempt diverting! Pray tell, why is the inn named The Ferry and Ferlie?"

"Doubtless you know what a ferry-boat is, Miss Bell? The flat, floating device normally utilized for conveying cattle, humanity and vehicles across a body of water?" He raised an enquiring brow.

"Do not be condescending, my lord, or I won't listen to your beastly horror story, which, I've no doubt, you're itching to tell!" she warned.

He laughed softly, the Gypsy eyes crinkling attractively. "Then I won't tease you. Suffice it to say that this inn has long been a stopping point for people wishing to cross the loch to the settlements on the other side. Just east of the road and directly opposite the inn's courtyard lies a stretch of beach ideal for launching boats. Such beaches are a scarcity along the shores of Loch Doon, because the loch is enclosed at most accessible points by steep, treacherous cliffs. Thus explains the first part of the inn's name." He paused, leaning slightly forward. "But do you have the vaguest notion what a ferlie is, Miss Bell?"

"No," she admitted, that pesky chill up her spine making another tingling appearance.

"It is an old Scots word for any sort of wonder or mysterious happening, most often used in describing ghosts, monsters, or beasties—as the Scots choose to call them—and all like creatures. And do you know why Mr. Stuart named his inn after such a thing as a ferlie?''

"N-no.''

"Because sightings of the loch monster have been reported more frequently in this area than at any other spot along the loch's miles of shoreline. I imagine it is because the beastie finds it difficult to heave his bulk atop the cliffs and chooses instead the sloping beach to sun himself. If I were thirty feet long and had as cumbersome a physique, I should choose to do the same thing,'' he observed philosophically.

"This is preposterous, Lord Hastings!'' Felicity exclaimed. "You don't imagine me such a gudgeon as to believe such a bouncer, do you?''

"You've heard of the Loch Ness monster, have you not, Miss Bell?''

"Everyone in Britain has heard of it,'' she retorted. "And I've seen Rowlandson's caricature drawing of the beast. He portrayed it in as ridiculous light as it deserves, I'm quite sure! 'Tis only a silly legend perpetuated by the ignorant!''

"Not all Nessie's visits have been to the uneducated, I assure you,'' the earl persisted, obviously enjoying himself. "Nor has the Loch Doon beast only disported himself within sight of the peasants, but he has been quite fair in giving frights to men and women at every level of education and society.''

"I suppose Mr. Stuart has regaled you with sundry accounts of the beastie's visits. Perhaps it knocked upon his door one night and beseeched a 'wee dram' before plunging to the depths of the cold loch!''

"No," answered the earl, "though the beastie was seen crossing the road about a mile north of here.''

"Who saw it, pray tell?" she challenged. "The village idiot?''

"The vicar saw it. Whether he's an idiot or not I cannot say," replied the earl with a grin.

Felicity was losing patience with the man. If he thought these ridiculous Banbury tales would cause her to fling herself into his arms for protection, *he* was the idiot!

"I still intend to sleep in the carriage, my lord. I shall feel vastly safer there than in any walled enclosure inhabited by the unclothed likes of you!" she retorted, flipping open her napkin with a decided snap and placing it on her lap. "Now where is dinner, I wonder. I'm starved!''

"Ah, I'm delighted to know your appetite is returning," he commented politely, making use of his own napkin. "And here is Sally at last." He smiled in the direction of the door and a comely maid entered the room balancing a trayful of dishes on one swaying hip and a basket of bread on the other. This did not seem to Felicity the most decorous way to serve food, and she eyed the girl suspiciously.

Sally placed the dishes on the table, never taking her eyes off Lord Hastings. He did not disappoint the flaxen-haired wench either, for he returned her besotted blue-eyed gaze with a wicked black one of his own, accompanied by a disarming smile. Felicity felt her ire rising. How dared he flirt so openly! If he did not take care, the foolish girl might spill a ladle of hot gravy on his lap. Mayhap that was just what was called for! she seethed.

Sally took an immoderate amount of time serving them, and then stood hovering over the table. Felicity was about to summarily dismiss the girl when Lord Hastings said, "Miss Bell, as long as we've got the daughter of the vicar's housekeeper in the room with us, perhaps you'd like to hear her account of the vicar's meeting with the beastie!"

"I'm quite sure Sally has duties in the kitchen she must attend to," Felicity replied dismissively. "I shouldn't wish the poor girl to have her ears boxed." *Unless I were boxing them,* thought Felicity.

"Oh, no, miss!" disclaimed the girl, the white swell of bosom above her low bodice jiggling with the fervour of her feelings. "I should like above anything to tell ye about it!"

"Proceed, Sally, my dear!" urged Lord Hastings, placing a steaming forkful of salmon into his mouth. Felicity supposed she'd no recourse but to listen to the ridiculous account of "the beastie that crossed the road," her appetite diminishing all the while, despite the splendid food in front of her.

"Vicar MacIan was comin' down the road from the village Dalmellington, just up the road, ye know, having jest been t'see the widow MacBean, mindin' his own business, so t'speak, when he saw a long neck, a wee bit thicker than an elephant's trunk . . .'' Sally paused for breath, the resulting intake of air threatening to send the white bosom spilling out of its restraining bodice entirely. Felicity shot a look in Lord Hastings's direction and felt a strong urge to slap the grin off his face.

''He dinna see the head, but the neck had three humps. And the vicar said that while it dinna slither like a snake, but rather heaved itself along, its skin was leathery like one of them reptiles and dark grey in colour. After the neck went by, there was a body shaped like a slug as tall as me, and as wide as it were tall!''

Sally was a petite girl, but the mere idea of a slug five feet high and just as wide, though it was only fictitious in nature, sent a shudder of revulsion through Felicity.

Lord Hastings noted the violent shudder, but only said, while peeling his boiled potato quite calmly, ''Thank you, Sally, for that riveting tale. Now, run along, my dear. I shan't be able to eat until you do, such a vision you are!''

This, of course, was a bold-faced lie. The earl had been eating all along. But Sally simpered and beamed and wiggled her hips in delight. Then, just as Sally turned to leave, Felicity noticed Lord Hastings's hand suspended in the air above the girl's shapely bottom. Had he not caught her astonished gaze, Felicity was quite sure the earl would have sent Sally off with a bawdy slap on the rump.

Once the servant-girl had closed the door behind her, Felicity could not help saying in the reproving voice of a fishwife, "*You* are the beastie, Lord Hastings! I wish you would restrain yourself a little! That girl was a mere child!"

The earl raised his brows. "Jealous, my dear Miss Bell? After all, I can hardly suppose you playing an act to convince the innkeeper and his servants of our relationship. We masquerade as brother and sister, not husband and wife!"

Felicity was too angry to reply. How dared he suggest she was jealous! She was embarrassed by his behaviour, that was all! A gentleman would not behave thusly!

"You ought to try the mushrooms, Miss Bell." He interrupted her murderous thoughts. "Mrs. Stuart has used just a touch of basil to bring out their savoury flavour."

Felicity remained silent, pushing her food about the plate in the sullen fashion of a scolded child. Presently her resentment of Lord Hastings's behaviour gave way to even more disturbing thoughts of...the "loch beastie." Of course she didn't for one minute believe it existed, but still the idea of sleeping in the carriage had lost a great deal of its appeal. If not a beastie, perhaps she'd be visited by a wolf, or a bear, or... Well, who knew what made its abode in these wild Scottish woods!

Finally the earl had finished his dinner. The only food left on the table were the cold lumps which reposed upon Felicity's barely touched plate. Lord Hastings sat back in his chair with the satisfied air of a completely happy man. No doubt he was well pleased with his vicious assault upon her nerves, thought Felicity. And now she must humble herself by admitting defeat! She'd share a room with the earl, all right, but if he so much as touched her, he'd find himself maimed for life! She busied her mind with the pleasant occupation of cataloguing all the various ways she might prolong the maiming process.

"We had better go to bed, Miss Bell."

Felicity's eyes jerked to the earl's face. His look was pure innocence.

"We may have a trying day ahead of us tomorrow. We'll be needing our rest tonight."

"Yes," she murmured, annoyed at the smile playing at the corners of the earl's mouth. She knew she was blushing. He probably found that amusing in a spinster like herself.

Then Lord Hastings's manner became businesslike. "You go first. I'll give you half an hour. Extinguish the candle and I'll undress in the dark. And, never fear, I shall be up and out of the room tomorrow morning before you've even opened your peepers."

Felicity stared wide-eyed at the earl. He was allowing her to back down gracefully! She didn't have to explain with bumbling ineptitude her very sensible reasons for changing her mind about sleeping in the carriage. He wasn't even gloating! In fact, he seemed determined not to cause her any discomfort at all. He avoided looking at her by fussing with his snuff-box, making a great show of stirring the aromatic mixture with a little shovel that had been stored inside.

Finally she prodded herself to movement. After all, he could not stir his snuff indefinitely. She had better take advantage of the dignified exit he was granting her. She stood up and walked to the door. Just as she was about to turn the knob she was seized by a most unwelcome sense of fair play. After all, he was being kind and thoughtful. Such behaviour ought to be rewarded. She turned.

"Lord Hastings?"

He lifted his head and cocked it slightly to the side. His look was indecipherable.

"G-good night," she stuttered.

He smiled. Felicity felt the warmth seep through her like a drenching summer's rain. Then he resumed his occupation with the snuff-box. "Good night, Miss Bell!"

Satisfied, she was turning to go when he spoke again. "By the by, Miss Bell, you *do* plan to sleep in the bed, don't you, not the cot?"

She stiffened and looked back at him. "If it doesn't inconvenience you, my lord."

"Not at all," he replied, lifting his glimmering black eyes to her face. "I only wanted to ascertain the sleeping arrangements for a certainty. It would not do to crawl in the wrong bed, now would it?"

Felicity's heart hammered violently against her rib cage. In this devil's estimation, was the wrong bed the one which she occupied, or the one which she didn't?

She left the parlour hastily, determined not to gratify the earl by responding to his baited remark. And to think she'd actually thought him being kind a minute ago!

Reaching her bedchamber, she threw off her clothes and splashed her face with water before flinging on her nightdress and flouncing into bed. Once she'd dug herself as deeply as possible into the bedcovers, clutching them with tight fists in a wad beneath her chin, she squeezed her eyes shut and lay perfectly still.

At least an hour passed before Felicity heard a key in the door. She hadn't been relaxed before, but now she stiffened to the rigidity of a twelve-month corpse, straining and flinching at every sound.

To his credit, Lord Hastings undressed with quiet consideration. But the infinitesimal sound of buttons being undone, the swish of cloth against cloth and the rustle of pantaloons descending to a pile on the floor was most disconcerting. Perhaps more so because Felicity's imagination was employing some rather vivid pictures of the earl's panther-like physique in instruction-book detail.

Finally he was undressed and settled in his cot, which, due to the smallness of the room, was a mere arm's length away. When his breathing became slower and more even, Felicity began to relax. She breathed a sigh of relief and turned onto her left side, towards the earl, which was her customary position for sleep.

"Never fear, Miss Bell," came a sleep-husky voice from out of the darkness. "I shall protect you from the loch beastie."

Felicity's eyes popped open. But who would protect her from the "cot beastie," or the beastie inside her that threatened to send her flying willingly into the earl's web of seduction?

CHAPTER FOUR

FELICITY AWOKE the next morning to bright sunlight flooding her room through the opened curtains and the sounds of splashing water. The chambermaid was dumping steaming bucketfuls into the copper tub Felicity had longed to become acquainted with the night before.

So, Lord Hastings was allowing her a bath, was he? But she would not try to analyse and be overly grateful for this latest kind gesture. She would simply enjoy it.

Felicity rose and bathed thoroughly, relishing every moment. The only thought to intrude and threaten to spoil her otherwise blissful bathe had to do with the size of the tub. It occurred to her that since she'd had difficulty arranging her own long limbs into the small confines of the copper tub, how on earth had Lord Hastings contrived to fit?

The resulting visual image of long, muscular legs dangling over the sides of the tub proved too disturbing for Felicity's peace of mind. She hastily completed her bath and vacated the tub, which had only hours before contained the perfectly naked Lord

Hastings. Then she changed into her green dress, which had been neatly cleaned and pressed.

Fortunately for Felicity's agitated nerves, she breakfasted alone. The earl had eaten early and had then joined his coachman in their inspection of the carriage wheels after their lengthy journey over muddy, rutted lanes. Though the sun shone, they would still have to endure an uncomfortable ride over the puddled roads.

Lord Hastings was all politeness as he helped Felicity into the carriage, and she might have endeavoured to forget the fact that they'd shared a bedchamber the night before if it were not for the glint of amusement still lurking in the depths of his black eyes. Felicity felt embarrassment envelop her as she recalled the sounds of his undressing and found herself unequal to idle chit-chat. Luckily, the earl did not press her into conversation and they travelled in silence.

Since the weather was so improved, Jenson rode outside with the coachman and Felicity sat opposite the earl, facing forward. The beautiful scenery eventually diverted her thoughts away from her embarrassment, and her nose was nearly pressed to the window in an effort to see as much as possible.

The road skimmed the shores of Loch Doon, and Felicity was fascinated by the dark, coffee-bean colour of its mirror-calm waters. She'd heard it said that Loch Ness was as deep as the North Sea, though how anybody could be sure of such a fact was beyond her understanding. Was Loch Doon as deep? she wondered.

Presently they left the loch behind and were surrounded by rolling green hills dotted with sheep. After a few hours, this scenery gave way to endless moors, the tranquil heather occasionally disturbed by a startled flock of reddish-brown grouse taking flight.

Lord Hastings had wisely guarded against the inevitable pangs of hunger by filling a napkin full of fruit. Felicity had no doubt that in the coming years a variety of fruit trees would spring up along the north road, merely from the seeding done by Lord Hastings. Cores from apples and pits from peaches were flung out of the carriage window on a regular basis.

Now and then, the earl drew her attention to some point of interest. Eventually Felicity grew much more comfortable in his company, since he behaved very pleasantly and did not once cast her a lecherous look.

Finally, after they'd eaten the lunch Mrs. Stuart had prepared for them, the road narrowed through a thick forest and the scent of the sea wafted through the open carriage window. A red deer, a magnificent stag with formidable antlers, struck a pose in a green meadow. Felicity was spellbound by the beauty surrounding her.

Presently Lord Hastings said, "Miss Bell, we are now within easy distance of Castle Culzean."

Felicity nodded, her throat tightening anxiously.

The woods thinned, and suddenly they were presented with a view which drew an appreciative gasp from Felicity. The sea, or more accurately, the Firth of Clyde, stretched out before them. High atop a cliff overlooking this magnificent body of sun-tipped waves was a huge, grey stone castle, its battlements creating a fortresslike silhouette against the azure blue of a late afternoon sky.

"What a beautiful, regal building!" Felicity exclaimed.

"The castle was designed by Robert Adam in the last century. The modern structure is built around a core of small chambers dating from the medieval period," Lord Hastings informed her.

Tooling up to the front courtyard, which faced away from the sea, they passed through lush, well-manicured grounds. Just opposite the front entryway was a large, artificial pond graced by a half-dozen beautiful black swans. In the center of the pond was an ornate fountain, displaying an angry-looking merman held up by several disgruntled fish, spewing water.

Lord Hastings had said that Kyle would be a rich man, but Felicity had hardly expected so much grandeur!

Finally the carriage jerked to a halt. At almost the same moment, a servant, whom Felicity presumed to be the butler, appeared at the castle door. While Lord Hastings disembarked, she observed the man with keen curiosity. The butler was very old, with white hair and beard. It seemed he held his rigid posture with difficulty, since from time to time he was obliged to pull himself up from an involuntary slump. His sloping shoulders were encased in a fitted jacket, and a tartan kilt revealed his bony knees. The kilt had a mix of colours that was similar, if not identical, to the tartan worn by the innkeeper's wife at Gretna Green.

Despite his infirmities of age, the butler presented a striking picture and was a fitting accessory for the grand house. His stern demeanour, however, was not the least welcoming.

"Goodness, if the butler is so easily able to blight me with a frosty look, how dare I face the marquess?" grumbled Felicity to herself.

"Did you say something, Miss Bell?" the earl enquired politely, extending his hand.

Felicity looked at the strong, brown hand and up into the black, teasing eyes. She blushed and mumbled, "No, nothing at all, Lord Hastings."

After the earl helped her from the carriage, Felicity wanted desperately to stretch her arms and legs, but dared not while the butler's gaze was upon them. Lord Hastings walked purposely forward, while she lagged behind with the leaden tread of a funeral marcher. The fierce-eyed ancient in the kilt seemed as ready to shoot them as give them the time of day.

"At ease, Geddes!" the earl loudly admonished as he walked up to within a foot of the butler. "It is I, Lord Hastings, with a guest! How I wish you'd invest in a lorgnette, old man, for how else can you discern friend from foe!''

So the butler was short-sighted, was he? And all along Felicity was sure he was watching her every move! And nearly deaf as well, for why else would Lord Hastings shout so?

At the sound of Lord Hastings's voice, the butler's eyes widened, then he squinted and peered closely at the earl. A large smile transformed his grim countenance. ''Master Jamie...er, my lord! We had'na thought t'see ye again so soon,'' he shouted back, which some elderly deaf people are prone to do. ''His lordship will be pleased! And ye've come right on the coattails of yer cousin!'' The butler squinted and smiled at Felicity. ''The lieutenant's brung a lass with him, too!''

''Where are they, Geddes?'' asked the earl.

''Pardon, my lord?'' queried the butler, cupping his ear.

''Where are they, Geddes?'' yelled the earl.

''In the parlour with his lordship,'' Geddes informed them, opening the door to admit them into the lofty hall. ''It has'na been more'n an hour since they come! Ye might as well ha'been travellin' together!''

''Goodness, I hardly supposed we were so close behind them!'' whispered Felicity. ''Maybe they spent the night in Dalmellington!''

''You needn't whisper, Miss Bell,'' observed Lord Hastings with a wry smile. ''Even if Geddes heard every word we said, I would not feel the least compunction in discussing family matters in front of him. He has been with the family since—"

"Since the medieval chambers were built?" Felicity suggested with a smile.

"Very probably," returned the earl, chuckling. "But as for Kyle and Susan, once we ascertained that they had no intention of marrying before they reached Culzean, it mattered little whether we caught up with them. I do not think Grandfather will marry them first thing. I doubt not he'll be as careful as you in discovering if they are suited to each other."

Felicity felt sure the earl had meant to reassure her, but by now, she was not as worried about Susan contracting an infelicitous marriage. Lately of a more practical frame of mind, she had been contemplating the difficulties Susan might endure if she *didn't* marry the lieutenant! After all, she'd jilted her betrothed (though he was still unaware he'd been jilted), and driven halfway across the country by a man she was not married to, and even stayed two nights in an inn with him. Unless it could all be kept mum—which, with the passing of time seemed less and less likely—Susan's reputation would be worthless.

At an excruciatingly slow pace, Geddes ushered them across the large, elegant hall and up a wide oak staircase to the drawingroom. Suppressing her impatience to see her sister, Felicity took note of the several portraits lining the walls. Theirs was a handsome family. And, most unusual, she'd not yet detected a fair-haired man in the whole bunch of them.

At last Geddes opened the drawingroom doors and announced Lord Hastings, but could in no wise announce Miss Bell, since he hadn't obtained her name. This caused the elderly butler a flustered moment, but he needn't have worried because two of the occupants of the room already knew the newcomer and pronounced her name in unison.

"Miss Bell!" exclaimed the lieutenant.

"Felicity!" cried Susan.

Paying no heed to the imposing presence of a tall, silver-haired gentleman standing by the lieutenant, Felicity walked quickly across the room towards her sister. Looking tiny and lost, Susan sat in a wing chair near the fireplace. Her slender face was as white as Lord Hastings's neckcloth. The expression of joy which lit Susan's eyes when she saw her sister erased any lingering doubts Felicity had about coming. Clearly Susan had need of her!

Susan rose to meet Felicity with outstretched arms. Unfortunately, she had quite forgot the cup of tea she'd been balancing on her lap. The delicate china crashed to the floor and a puddle of tea spread across the beautiful Oriental carpet.

"Susan! Look what you've d—" Felicity stopped mid-reproof. Susan would be mortified enough without a scold from her older sister. But Susan seemed oblivious to the accident and by some miracle of chance stepped over the broken pieces without piercing the sole of her slipper. However, she did step directly in the enlarging pool of tea, leaving dainty brown footsteps on the cream-and-blue carpet behind her as she closed the distance between them.

Good heavens, thought Felicity as she embraced Susan, *what will Lord Ailsa think of such a display?* And first meetings generally made lasting impressions! But Susan must have been terribly nervous, because generally she realized when she'd had an accident and was quick though embarrassed to offer her apologies. There was no sign of either about to take place.

All at once pandemonium broke out. Lord Hastings loudly apprised Geddes of the accident, since the butler had neither seen nor heard it happen. Geddes shuffled down the hall, bellowing for the chambermaid. The lieutenant apologized to his grandfather for the mess and assured him that Susan was not usually so clumsy, and, at the same time, greeted Lord Hastings after a two-year separation with a brief but thorough embrace, then demanded to know how the devil he had met up with Miss Bell.

Intermingled with Kyle's excited Scottish brogue were the gruff, clipped tones of his grandfather's and Lord Hastings's soothing baritone. Irrelevantly, Felicity thought their blended voices sounded rather melodic. That they sounded musical notwithstanding, she wished they'd lower their voices so her task of calming Susan would be made easier.

Felicity pulled Susan to sit down beside her on a sofa and explained as briefly as possible how she came to be there with Lord Hastings. At the same time, Lord Hastings offered explanations to Kyle and his grandfather.

Some ten minutes later everyone was reasonably in possession of the facts, the worst of the accident had been removed and repaired and Susan belatedly blushed.

"How clumsy of me! How *dreadfully* clumsy of me!" she moaned in her breathy little voice.

"Blether!" soothed the lieutenant, who'd sat down on the other side of Susan and was stroking her hand. "Ye received a shock when yer sister entered the room. 'Tis perfectly understandable that ye forgot yer tea. Dinna fret now, love."

But Susan would not be comforted. She looked perilously close to tears. And it did not help that Lord Ailsa was staring at her from beneath his heavy, dark brows. Such a stare would make even the most composed, self-assured young lady fall to pieces! Felicity's protective instincts prompted her to draw Lord Ailsa's attentions to herself.

"While Lord Hastings's explanation included mention of who I am, Lord Ailsa, we haven't been properly introduced, have we?" she said, forcing an engaging smile to her lips.

"Nor have we!" agreed Lord Ailsa, fixing his keen black-eyed gaze on her instead of Susan. "How do ye do, Miss Bell?" Like Lord Hastings, Lord Ailsa's most riveting feature was his dark, luminous eyes. They were all the more striking, too, because while his hair and thick moustache were silver, his brows were a rich, smoky grey. Indeed, to be the object of his attention brought goose bumps to Felicity's arms. And what a tall, imposing figure he was in his kilt, vest and shirt-sleeves, even though he must be going on eighty years! They were a family of goliaths, these Kennedys!

"I am not usually so remiss in proper attentions to my guests, Miss Bell, but..."

"Indeed, you certainly did not expect guests, did you?" she said apologetically.

"It has been a day of surprises," he admitted ruefully, his scowling gaze returning to Susan. "I must confess, I'm still a wee bit puzzled over certain details."

"Kyle and I will readily supply you with details, Grandfather," Lord Hastings offered. "But the ladies must be fagged to death after their tedious journeys. If they retire to their rooms now, they will have just enough time for a nap before dinner."

Lord Ailsa turned and seemed to eye his English grandson suspiciously, but he only said, "Aye, Jamie, ye're right." Then he pulled the bellcord hanging near the fireplace and a footman appeared at the door. "Fetch Geddes," he ordered. The footman immediately departed to tell the butler he'd been summoned.

Felicity felt sure the butler must have been held in considerable affection or he'd have certainly been pensioned off by now. She settled back against the sofa cushions in expectation of a rather lengthy wait for Geddes.

Since Lord Hastings had conveniently engaged the lieutenant and Lord Ailsa in an engrossing political conversation, and Susan was weak and mute from fright and exhaustion, Felicity took the opportunity to have a more thorough look at her surroundings.

The room was circular in design, with several tall windows facing the sea. Since the windows came nearly to the floor, even from her seat across the room Felicity had an excellent view of the waters below.

Her guidebook had explained that the Firth of Clyde had a distinguishing feature, that being a rather beautiful island. And there it was. Like the jagged teeth of a granite monster, the peaks and ridges of the Isle of Arran thrusted mightily to the sky. Felicity could just imagine the sun setting behind such a spectacular piece of rock, which seemed to have been dropped by pure accident into the middle of the firth.

Dragging her eyes reluctantly from the window, she continued to study the room. The furniture was light and elegant, the marble fireplace classic Adam. In fact, she could see the Robert Adam genius for design in every corner of the room...

"Good heavens!"

"What is it?" Lord Hastings was politely attentive. The gentlemen's conversation ended abruptly and all eyes were upon her. But Felicity was too enthralled to be intimidated.

"Look!" she said, pointing to a large, full-length portrait hanging above the fireplace.

The earl obeyed, though he'd apparently seen the picture many times before. In fact, he must have posed for it.

"It...it's you, my lord!" stammered Felicity, struck forcefully by the breath-catching magnificence of the picture.

"No, 'tisn't me," the earl informed her, an amused smile tugging at the corners of his mouth.

But who else could it be? thought Felicity. There was no mistaking those black eyes, the winged brows, the jet black hair (though in this case, it was pulled back and tied with a ribband), and the tall, muscular figure. Dressed in a plumed hat, green fitted jacket with gold trim, a kilt falling to the middle of his knees and with tartan stockings clinging to his muscular calves, this glorious man could be none other than Lord Hastings.

Felicity studied the picture, mesmerized, once or twice snatching a look at Lord Hastings as if she were comparing features. "It must be you!" she declared at last. "Lieutenant Kennedy, surely your cousin is hoaxing me." She turned appealing eyes to the lieutenant.

"Nay, Miss Bell, 'tisn't Jamie," concurred the lieutenant.

"Then who is it?" demanded Felicity.

"The portrait is of me in my prime, Miss Bell!" said Lord Ailsa.

"But of course!" exclaimed Felicity. "How stupid of me! Isn't that amazing! The family resemblance is remarkable. There, Lord Hastings, now you know exactly how you shall look when you are an old—" Felicity gasped and slapped her hand over her mouth. Even Susan gasped, apparently dumbfounded to discover her older sister equally capable of embarrassing herself. But Lord Ailsa's response was completely unexpected. He laughed.

It was a deep-timbred laugh, and seemed to rumble up from the toes of his black buckled slippers to the tip of his silver head. Felicity and Susan sat openmouthed, hardly believing the formidable marquess capable of such a delightful sound.

"Ye're a feisty lass, aren't ye, Miss Bell?" suggested Lord Ailsa with something like admiration in his black eyes.

Felicity wanted to say that Susan was feisty, too. That feistiness ran in the family, and that if he would only laugh more and scowl less, maybe Susan would grow brave enough to reveal her own special sort of feistiness. But she didn't. The words caught in her throat under the spell of Lord Ailsa's piercing eyes. Drat the man! Drat him and both his grandsons!

"Ye summoned me, my lord?" Geddes had finally arrived and was hollering from the drawing-room threshold.

"Yes, Geddes," replied his lordship in thundering tones. "Are the ladies' rooms ready?"

"Aye, my lord!"

"Then send Mrs. Rose, Geddes!"

"Aye, my lord!"

Mrs. Rose, a short, plumpish matron with a large ring of keys hanging from one of her apron strings, came to lead them to their rooms.

The lieutenant bade Susan an endearing goodbye and sent her off with a parting look of tender eloquence. This lovers' adieu was in striking contrast to the last look exchanged between Felicity and Lord Hastings. The twinkle in his black eyes suggested that he'd like to give her a pinch, or perhaps a sound slap on the rear. She scowled at him. Couldn't he see that this was no time for flirtatious levity! Indeed, it was highly improper that he look at her in such a way under any circumstance! The beastie!

But once the drawingroom doors were shut behind them, Felicity couldn't help but smile. And as she smiled, a little of the tension built up over the past several minutes eased away.

AS THE DOORS CLOSED, a new sort of tension gripped the gentlemen. Now that the ladies had gone, Lord Ailsa could speak as plainly as he chose. And he chose to speak plainly indeed.

"By God, Kyle, ye're still bringing home the lost lamb, aren't ye!"

Kyle stiffened. "Grandfather, bringing Susan to Culzean can hardly be compared to my childhood propensity for picking up stray animals. I mean to marry her."

"So ye've said, lad," growled the marquess. "And by the strict Sassenach rules, if ye dinna marry her now after bringing her so far, she'd be ruined."

"That is beside the point, sir," Kyle returned emphatically. "I love her!"

"Lad, she's the first English-speaking lass ye clapped yer eyes on after the war. Can ye be in love as fast that?" reasoned Lord Ailsa. "Mayhap it's something else ye feel for the lass."

Kyle turned livid. Lord Hastings could see that intervention, loath though he was to meddle, was in order.

"Grandfather, surely you can have nothing against the girl! She comes of an excellent family—I think! And pray tell, how long did it take you to fall in love with Grandmother?"

Lord Hastings could tell he'd scored a palpable hit. But his grandfather presently recovered, saying, "Yer grandmother was a Scot, Jamie!"

"Don't say you hold Susan's English blood against her, Grandfather. My father was a Sassenach and you and he were as thick as thieves."

Lord Ailsa sighed heavily. "Ye dinna understand, Jamie. Kyle will be chieftain. He needs a strong lass.

He needs a lass who'll hold the clan traditions as dear to her heart as he does.''

"*Susan* is precisely what I need!" insisted Kyle. "And if ye'd give her but half a chance... She's a gentle creature, Grandfather! Perhaps if ye weren't so gruff..."

"I am what I am, Kyle," Lord Ailsa stated, uncompromising.

"If ye'll not marry us, Grandfather, we'll just find ourselves a couple of witnesses and—"

"I dinna say I would'na marry ye, Kyle!" Lord Ailsa said in a low, gruff tone.

"Well then, for God's sake, why are ye making such a fuss?" Kyle implored impatiently.

Lord Ailsa moved to stand directly in front of Kyle. He gripped him by the shoulders. "Ye must be sure, lad. Ye'll be shackled to the lass for life."

Kyle stood taller and looked his grandfather straight in the eye. "I've never been more sure of anything in my life."

Lord Ailsa could be no proof against such confidence. Lord Hastings certainly wasn't. He was struck to the soul by Kyle's sincerity. Would that he could be as sure of a woman! But thus far in his chequered career dealing with the petticoat line, he'd found women to be more problematic than otherwise. To repose complete confidence in a woman, to offer your whole heart to be treasured or trampled, seemed foolhardy to Lord Hastings. He had much rather keep his heart to himself, thank you very much!

Lord Ailsa walked away from Kyle and stood by the window, looking out over the beautiful sea-scape. Kyle and Lord Hastings waited silently for their grandfather to speak. "I'd planned a celebration for yer homecoming, Kyle, a gathering of the clan. The date set is four days hence. Can ye wait that long to wed the lass?"

"Aye, Grandfather," Kyle answered. "But no longer."

"Then so be it," Lord Ailsa pronounced resignedly.

But now a pall fell over the room. The determination of a wedding date ought to be a festive occasion, thought Lord Hastings. Rather it seemed as if they were planning a funeral! Kyle stood awkwardly in the middle of the room, as if he didn't know what to do or how to feel. Indeed, he'd won his heart's desire; he'd convinced Grandfather to wed them. But how much more glad he might feel if only Grandfather approved of his choice! Lord Hastings felt for him exceedingly.

He felt for Lord Ailsa, too, Surely this rift between them was not what he'd expected from Kyle's long-awaited homecoming.

"ARE YOU FEELING MORE the thing, dearest?" Felicity had gone with Susan to her bedchamber and had just tucked her into bed for a nap.

"Yes, Felicity," sighed Susan, nestling her head against the pillow. "How glad I am that you are here!"

"Rest now. You must be very tired from your long journey. I know I am!"

"Ah, but the journey up here was wonderful," breathed Susan, her hazel eyes softening dreamily. "I love being with Kyle!" Then her face crumpled. "But I had not expected his grandfather to be so dreadfully stern. He obviously disapproves of me. Every time he looks at me, I feel as if I shall sink to the floor in a quivering heap!"

"But he can't disapprove of you. He hardly knows you," insisted Felicity.

"He knows I'm a clumsy clodpole!"

"The only complaint Lord Ailsa can possibly have at this point is that you aren't Scottish. Therein lies the crux of the matter. As for the other..." Felicity waved her hands in an airy dismissal of the broken china and stained Oriental carpet. "It does not signify one jot. Once you are more composed, you'll regain your natural agility. You know I'm right."

"If he keeps glaring at me in such a way I shall never be composed in his company!" said Susan, with a slight sniff.

"Here's my advice to you. Whenever he glowers at you, imagine him as he would appear in his nightdress and cap. Then he'll not seem nearly so dignified and forbidding!"

Susan giggled. "Felicity! Dare I?"

Felicity smiled. "Why not? Who shall know what you are thinking besides me?" Then, in a more serious tone, "If you love Kyle and mean to be the best wife possible, you must learn to fit in here, Susan. And that means rubbing along well with Lord Ailsa." She hesitated. "Are you quite sure you love Kyle, Susan, and are not just...well...avoiding other things, like Wenthorp, or...Henry?"

Again Susan's face took on that dreamy quality. Her voice was soft and full of conviction. "I never thought it possible to love someone as I love Kyle. Before, I would have married Wenthorp just to please Henry and avoid another Season, and fancy myself reasonably happy. But now I know what real happiness is, Felicity!"

Felicity was convinced that Susan knew what real happiness was. Her glowing countenance testified to her love for Kyle, and Felicity could rest easy about that particular worry. Now, if only Lord Ailsa could be brought round!

Felicity left Susan sleeping and went to her own room. She longed for a nap herself, but she had letters to write. Henry must be made aware of the situation so that he could break the news of Susan's elopement to Wenthorp. Aunt Mathilda, too, must be assured of their safety and informed that Felicity would be staying at the castle until Susan was married. Felicity hoped that tonight she would discover exactly when that would be.

Since she'd left a letter for Hugo with the inn-keeper at Gretna Green, there was no need to write to him. Felicity calculated that Hugo ought to be arriving at the castle sometime tomorrow.

Felicity's bedchamber contained a lovely escritoire which had been placed in a sunny window alcove. The window faced the formal grounds and Felicity was frequently tempted from her writing task to look out at the view. Three black swans floated in a languid circle, round and round the mossy pond. And the thickening woods beyond the formal grounds promised cool repose, the breeze-fluttered leaves of the trees flashing in the sunlight like gewgaws on a ladybird.

Shaking her head to clear it of such fanciful flights, Felicity doggedly returned to her letters. She had to be sure to word them carefully so as not to alarm either Henry or Aunt Mathilda, since she had no wish to complicate matters by their appearing on the castle steps.

She supposed Lord Hastings would be leaving for England at the first opportunity. He'd said he had business to attend to. Now that he had gallantly escorted her over the danger-fraught north roads—had done what he perceived as his duty—he had no reason to remain. Unless, of course, he was of a mind to attend Kyle's wedding.

Felicity brushed the quill of her writing pen across the curve of her chin, frowning. He was an arrogant, high-handed man! And she strongly suspected he was a seasoned rake. She ought to be glad to see the back of him. Thank goodness she was no silly, romantical schoolroom miss, or else those black eyes would be the undoing of her. At her advanced age, she was immune to the blatant flirtatious flummery employed by Lord Hastings. Still, he had a certain way of looking at her that . . .

Never mind! thought Felicity, calling herself firmly to order. Then, dipping her pen in the well, she began, "Dear Aunt Mathilda . . ."

CHAPTER FIVE

AFTER HER BATH, Felicity was assisted by one of the chambermaids to dress for dinner. She was beginning to loathe the three gowns she'd brought on the journey. It was tedious switching them about continually, wearing one while another was being cleaned and pressed. And it was no use borrowing from Susan's wardrobe, since her sister's gowns would be both short in length and insufficient through the bodice.

Tonight Felicity wore the rose sarcenet. It was a little more formal than the other two, and she needed all her confidence about her if she was going to withstand the piercing eyes of Lord Ailsa.

As it happened, the chambermaid, Meg, had a talent for dressing hair, and urged Felicity to allow her the privilege of styling such a glorious mass of titian curls. When Meg was through, Felicity was amazed with the result. She had a froth of curls at her crown, and delicate, loosely coiled tendrils danced all round her face. She would not blush to be thusly coiffured in even the most distinguished London drawingroom.

Felicity thanked the chambermaid warmly and left the room imbued with the extra confidence a woman feels when she knows she's in her best looks.

That she hoped Lord Hastings might find her attractive tonight was a possibility Felicity firmly suppressed. He might flirt, but she strongly doubted that he had any serious intentions. Besides, she quite cherished her independence, and Lord Hastings was nothing if not a headstrong man, bent on having his own way in all matters. Even if she were disposed to marry, which she wasn't, his sort would never do for *her!* She endeavoured to put the earl out of her mind.

As she walked along the gallery to Susan's room, she examined the family portraits hanging on the wall. She noted again that without exception the men had dark hair. She was staring up at one of the portraits depicting a man and his wife against a pastoral background when she was surprised by Lord Hastings's voice. What a silent tread he had, rather like a panther, for she'd no notion he was standing beside her until he spoke!

"That is a picture of my great-grandfather and great-grandmother," he said. "She was a bonny lass, wasn't she?"

Was it her imagination, or did Lord Hastings slip into a bit of a Scottish burr from time to time since they'd arrived at the castle? She slid her eyes away from the portrait and fixed them on the earl, half expecting him to be arrayed in full Scottish regalia, just as in the portrait of his grandfather. But his black jacket and pantaloons, pearl brocade vest and blindingly white shirt and neckcloth were quite elegant and indisputably English. Beau Brummel could not have turned himself out better.

The only criticism the Beau might have would be that Lord Hastings wore his hair too long. But Felicity rather liked the way the thick black waves curled against his collar.

"To tell truth, my lord," answered Felicity, in a light voice calculated to assure the earl that his elegant appearance did not daunt her in the least, "I was rather more enthralled with the gentleman! What a prodigious quantity of black waving hair, and that mustache—so trim and dapper, and twirled at the ends!"

Lord Hastings laughed softly. "He'd a bit of vanity, I'm sure."

Felicity was about to saucily suggest that perhaps vanity was a family tradition, but her sense of fairness stopped her. While he might be justly tempted to think well of himself and his handsome face and figure, Lord Hastings did not carry on like a coxcomb. But to concede that the earl lacked for vanity seemed to suggest that he deserved her admiration. It was too confusing!

Felicity pressed on with the conversation. "I'm amazed that all the men have dark hair, ranging from a rich mahogany to, er, *your* particular colour. I should have thought that somewhere along the line another shade might have surfaced!"

"Ah, but it is a long-standing trait amongst the Kennedy men, Miss Bell," replied Lord Hastings. "In fact the name Kennedy is derived from the Celtic *ceann dubh,* meaning black-headed." He took her elbow and guided her farther along the gallery.

"And here is a portrait of my cousin, Dominus, who raised a fencible regiment in 1745, eight hundred strong, in nine days. The men were so tall that there was no light company, nearly three hundred of them being upwards of six feet in height!"

"I have observed the exceptional height of your family," agreed Felicity rather breathlessly, his hand on her elbow causing her pulse to speed. Lord Hastings smiled approvingly, as if he was pleased that Felicity was interested in his genealogy.

"And here—"

"Oh, Felicity! There you are!"

Susan was walking down the hall towards them, and she was doing so with perfect grace. Felicity's heart swelled with pride at the lovely picture her sister presented in her blue sprigged gown and the dainty matching slippers peeking out from beneath the flounced hem. Felicity turned to the earl. "There, you see! Susan is not always so clum—"

But she spoke too soon. Susan's face registered alarm at something or someone farther down the hall behind them. Suddenly the dainty slippers appeared to tangle about her feet and Susan fell, face forward and with a resounding thump, to the floor. She toppled with such force that even her silky auburn hair was loosened by the jolt and hairpins sprayed the hall.

"Good God, Miss Bell, are you quite all right?"

Lord Hastings stooped to assist Susan to her feet, while Felicity turned to look down the hall. Just as she suspected, Lord Ailsa was approaching them from the opposite end. If the mere sight of Lord Ailsa had so discomposed Susan, this did not bode well for the rest of the evening! Felicity sighed and proceeded to pick up Susan's hairpins. Susan had need of another remonstration!

"Oh, dear, so clumsy of me!" mumbled Susan, her flushed face almost hidden beneath a mane of dishevelled hair. "How kind of you, Lord Hastings! But I'm perfectly all right!"

"Come along, dear—we'd best return to your room and repair the damage," said Felicity, trying hard to subdue her exasperation. After all, Susan couldn't seem to help herself.

Turning to Lord Hastings, Felicity whispered, "Please explain to your grandfather and Lieutenant Kennedy that we shall be slightly detained for dinner!" Then Felicity hustled her sister back to her room before Susan could be further upset by the look of disapproval she was sure would be on Lord Ailsa's face.

DINNER WAS DELICIOUS. The many courses included fresh salmon marinated in lemon juice and coriander, lobster and crab in a citrus vinaigrette, scallops,

pigeon breast in a red wine sauce fragrant with ju-
niper berries, lamb fillet, tender and flavoured with
fresh mint, perfectly aged cheeses and numerous
side-dishes of fresh garden vegetables and fruit.

Felicity was overwhelmed by the quantity and
quality of food set before her. So tempting was the
colourful and savoury array that she managed to eat
a substantial meal for the first time in three days,
despite her continued anxiety for Susan.

As for Susan, she must have completely forgotten
the advice Felicity had repeated to her following her
tumble in the hall. After all, how could she imagine
Lord Ailsa in nightdress and cap if she would not
even look at him? And now his few gruff attempts to
converse with Susan were answered in such a small,
trembling voice that Lord Ailsa presently gave up
and concentrated on his dinner.

Felicity examined the situation. Lord Ailsa sat at
the head of the table with Susan at his right, while
Felicity was seated at his left. Susan was directly
across the table from her. But recommending aloud
to her sister that she have done with acting like a wet
goose did not seem to Felicity to be the wisest of action. And obtaining Susan's attention might be little
difficult, as well, since besides staring blankly at her
plate, she had eyes and conversation for Kyle only.

With sudden inspiration, Felicity decided to give
her sister a gentle kick under the table. Once she'd
got her attention, perhaps Felicity might be able to
convey her message by raising a meaningful brow.

She stretched her right leg beneath the table, positioning it just so. She was fortunate to have very long legs and was certain of making contact with one of her sister's shins.

Then, with all the appearance of innocence and while delicately dabbing her mouth with a napkin, she took aim and thrust her foot forward. Felicity's gratification at making contact the first time was immediately curtailed when Lord Ailsa cried out in pain. She'd kicked the wrong person!

"Demme!" Lord Ailsa's outburst and his sudden jerk, which splashed wine on his neckcloth, took them all by surprise. Startled eyes flew to where he sat. While he'd said precious little for the past several minutes, no one expected him to break his silence with a curse! Since Susan's relative composure had hinged on the marquess's silence, she trembled with renewed fear.

In truth, Felicity trembled as well. Her guilt must have been reflected in her face, not to mention the incriminating closeness of their seating arrangement. Lord Ailsa glanced first at Susan and seemed to recoil at the fear evident on her face, then settled his gaze on Felicity.

Felicity decided her best course was to brazen it out. She would hide her apprehension and return his lordship's gaze, bold as brass. She hadn't meant to kick him, and she'd certainly underestimated the strength of her thrust. But she regretted the pain she'd afflicted, and her look was probably more apologetic than bold.

Piercing black eyes locked with clear, unwavering green. Felicity was relieved to discover a hint of amusement shining in the black depths of Lord Ailsa's eyes.

"Beg pardon, ladies," he said at length. "Bit of the rheumatics in my calf." He leaned forward and stretched his arm beneath the tablecloth, evidently rubbing the afflicted appendage. "Comes on me of a sudden, ye know," he explained.

Felicity flashed Lord Ailsa a grateful smile. When he returned her a fleeting, covert grin before attending to his sullied neckcloth, she began to hope that his sense of humour and tolerance might be extended to include Susan. But Susan would not inspire these feelings in the marquess if she continued to act so hen-hearted.

Felicity had returned to her dinner, her mind racing with possible ways to help her sister, when she had the disconcerting suspicion that she was being observed. Lord Hastings sat to her left, but since Felicity had been so involved in observing Susan, she'd positively ignored him. Actually she had tried very hard to ignore him. He was much too distracting for her own peace of mind. But now she was compelled by those persistent black eyes to pay him a little attention.

He had been just as quiet as his grandfather during the meal, and now he lifted his brows quizzically, his Gypsy eyes alight with speculation. She had no doubt he meant to ruthlessly question her later.

After dinner, Felicity and Susan left the gentlemen to their port and whisky and removed to the drawingroom. But, judging by the pained look on Kyle's face when Susan was compelled to leave his side for the sake of a foolish male tradition, Felicity felt sure they would not linger long at the dining table.

"I thought I'd fall into a swoon when Lord Ailsa cursed at the table," confided Susan, settling herself into a comfortable chaise. "Indeed his rheumatics must be of the most painful variety!"

"He hadn't the rheumatics," Felicity bluntly revealed. "I kicked him!"

"You what?" squeaked Susan, gaping at her sister as she sat down beside her.

"I didn't mean to kick him," explained Felicity, arranging her skirts. "I meant to kick you."

Though it hardly seemed possible, Susan's voice went up another octave. "Me? Pray tell, Felicity, why would you wish to kick me? I thought you loved me!"

"Indeed, I do love you, Susan" was Felicity's severe answer, "but you persist in playing the pudding-heart! I meant to remind you of that by kicking you under the table. You mustn't let Lord Ailsa's stern looks put you in such a twitter, dearest. He can't help looking stern, and he won't eat you, you know!"

Susan's eyes welled with tears. "I can't help the way I feel, either! Indeed, Felicity, you haven't the slightest notion of what it's like to be frightened of someone. I daresay you were born with all the bravery between us! Besides, he doesn't disapprove of *you.* You aren't marrying his precious grandson!" She dashed away a tear, saying, "Where *is* my reticule. I have need of a handkerchief!"

Felicity was feeling a little ashamed of herself. She really had ought to tread gently when dealing with Susan!

She cast her eyes about for Susan's reticule and discovered it lay on a nearby table. She fetched the bag and handed it to Susan. But Susan was blinded by tears and groped unsuccessfully through the copious contents of the reticule for her handkerchief. Felicity watched as long as she could, then she plucked the bag from her sister's hands and dumped it upside-down on the chaise. She found the desired handkerchief and handed it to Susan, then proceeded to put everything back.

"What is this?" In the midst of every sort of feminine essential, such as a vial of sal volatile, a hairbrush, a beaded pouch to carry pin-money, several hairpins and a glove, Felicity had discovered a small printed picture, about six inches wide and four inches tall. But before she could examine it thoroughly, Susan had snatched it from her hand and hid it behind her back.

"Good heavens, Susan!" laughed Felicity. "What have you got there?"

Susan's eyes had shed their tears and were wide and alert. "Promise you won't scold?" she wheedled.

Felicity's eyebrows lifted. "Such a request naturally awakens suspicion, my dear sister! Ought you to be scolded?"

"No, I ought not to be scolded!" Susan insisted. Then she sighed and brought the mysterious picture from behind her back. "But you must judge for yourself, I suppose," she finished, handing it to Felicity.

The picture appeared to be a print on the order of Gillray's or Rowlandson's famous caricatures, which could be purchased at various novelty shops round London. The realistically coloured drawing depicted Scots in kilts with several promenading women nearby. The Scots were part of His Majesty's Highlander troops. By the inscription at the bottom, Felicity immediately perceived that it was a print produced in France. She read the French inscription and learned that the troops thus depicted were fashioned after those which occupied Paris after the battle of Waterloo.

The men were a dashing sight in their high-plumed hats and red jackets! However, the astonished expressions on the women's faces as they watched the kilted militia carry out war exercises was what made the picture truly remarkable. The source of this astonishment was clearly depicted as each soldier filing past exposed a glimpse of bare backside as his kilt flipped and rippled in the breeze!

"Susan, where did you find this picture?" exclaimed Felicity, amused and appalled at the same time. "And why did you purchase it?"

"I don't remember exactly what shop it was! But I couldn't resist buying it." Susan's smile made her appear shy and mischievous at the same time. "I think it vastly diverting! Don't you?"

Felicity was flabbergasted to discover a side of Susan she'd never suspected. "I suppose," she admitted cautiously. "But it's a bit fast. You haven't shown it to anyone else, have you?"

Susan simpered. "Only Kyle."

"Kyle? Good heavens, Susan!" exclaimed Felicity. "That seems coming in a young lady! Was Kyle shocked?"

"Why should he be? There are no reservations between me and Kyle," Susan replied matter-of-factly. Then the mischievous glint in her eyes returned. "And *do* be honest, Felicity, when you see a man in a kilt don't you wonder what he's wearing underneath, or if he's wearing anything at all?"

The thought had crossed Felicity's mind, rather more frequently of late. "Yes, but it was never a consuming curiosity," she replied evasively, setting the scandalous print on the rosewood table next to the chaise.

"Why, Felicity, you're blushing," teased Susan. Then Susan clasped Felicity's hands and looked her in the eye. "I will tell you, sister!" she said in a low, confiding voice. "Unless they choose to wear nothing at all, most Scots wear short, close-fitting breeches called trews. And they are just as colourful as the kilt itself!"

Felicity was dismayed! Had Susan and Kyle become intimate on the trip? If so, it was more crucial than ever that Susan's marriage to Kyle be accomplished without further delay! Though Lord Ailsa had said at dinner that the wedding was to be in four days' time, Felicity would not be satisfied until the actual ceremony was concluded!

"I gather you extracted this information from some Scottish tome you borrowed from the lending library?" Felicity suggested carefully, hoping against hope that Susan had overcome her firmly entrenched aversion to reading.

Susan had the grace to blush. "No," she replied, laughing nervously. "Kyle, er, told me!"

Though she might be slightly aghast at the intimate nature of Susan's conversation with Kyle, Felicity hoped her sister was telling the truth. She had much rather Kyle told Susan what he wore beneath his kilt than shown her! But the seeds of doubt were planted, and now Felicity must wonder and worry over yet another aspect of her sister's relationship with Kyle.

Just then the gentlemen entered the room. Felicity instinctively sought Lord Hastings. She had a strong urge to confide in him. Their eyes locked and Felicity got the distinct impression that he, too, wished to speak to her. Kyle and Susan met in the middle of the floor and floated wordlessly to a distant corner. Lord Hastings crossed the room and stood beside the chaise Felicity occupied, declining Lord Ailsa's invitation to sit down.

"I am stiff with sitting and lying down," said the earl. "In fact I think I rather fancy a walk. Don't you, Miss Bell?"

Felicity was in a quandary. One part of her wanted to confide in Lord Hastings, and he was obviously giving her the opportunity by suggesting a walk. The other part of her dreaded the intimacy of walking unescorted with the earl. Her eyes drifted nervously to the windows where the muted, golden glow of twilight filtered through the glass. A soft breeze lifted the sheer draperies by an open window and the seductive, come-hither scent of summer's eve teased Felicity's senses.

"Well?" prompted the earl.

Those eyes, thought Felicity. *Those blasted Gypsy eyes!* She ought to refuse. She *must* refuse!

Convinced, Felicity opened her mouth to decline Lord Hastings's most civil invitation, when Lord Ailsa picked up Susan's French print from off the rosewood table by the chaise and studied it with interest.

Good heavens, thought Felicity, *how could I have been so careless!* Then, hoping to save her sister from falling further from his lordship's graces, Felicity decided to claim the picture as her own. She exclaimed, "Oh, Lord Ailsa! Do please give me back my print. I did not mean for *you* to see it! I only meant it as a joke to share with my sister! She did not much like it, though. She is very refined!"

But instead of taking offence, Lord Ailsa laughed aloud! "Ye're a saucy one, Miss Bell!" he said, returning the picture to her outstretched hand, but not before Lord Hastings had snatched a look at it. "I like a lass with a taste for humour!"

He smiled down at her with such warmth that Felicity hardly knew what to do! Could she tell him now that the print really belonged to Susan? Might he believe her to be fabricating in order to help Susan win favour in his eyes? Which was exactly what she had originally intended, but with opposite results! Felicity sat silently, miserably aware that she'd made a bumblebath of things!

Apparently Lord Hastings sensed her dilemma and leaned down to slide his hand under Felicity's elbow. "Come, Miss Bell," he commanded. "I've rather an urgent need for some fresh air. Walk with me!" He bobbed his head at Lord Ailsa. "You'll excuse us, won't you, Grandfather?" Lord Ailsa nodded his permission.

Though the earl's manner was brusque, at this point Felicity had no thoughts of refusing him. She turned to take her leave from her sister, but discovered Susan immersed in low and secret conversation with her fiancé. Felicity knew she would not be missed by them.

"We shall return shortly, my lord," she called back to him as she was propelled hastily to the drawingroom doors. Lord Ailsa bowed his head in answer, a keen look in his eyes and a smile on his lips. It was a devilish smile, just like Lord Hastings's!

LORD HASTINGS inhaled a cleansing breath of salty air. It felt good to be outside in the sweet stillness of a Scottish twilight. Half day, half night, it seemed the sun would hover at the horizon forever.

"Oh, it's lovely out here!" exclaimed Felicity, her face turned towards the sea.

Lord Hastings had settled Felicity's arm in the crook of his elbow. It was a pleasant sensation to have her attached to him thusly—the baggage! He shifted round so that they both faced the sea. Scattered streaks of clouds, radiant scarlet and gold, accompanied by the stone-glint of the Isle of Arran were breathtaking. Let her enjoy the sunset now, he thought, for in a few minutes she'll be wishing me at Jericho and bent on returning to the castle!

He turned so that they were strolling along the walkway which led through the castle grounds. They walked silently for a time, past the pond where the swans dipped and drifted on its calm surface, and past the orangery.

"Where are we going?" she asked him as they approached the end of the gravelled walk. He thought she trembled as he led her down the footpath which twined through the forest.

"To the loch," he answered calmly. He did not wish her to bolt just yet. He had much to say.

"Is there a lake so close to the castle?"

"Yes."

"Oh." She fell silent.

"I love this time of the evening," Felicity presently observed, a soft sigh parting her lips.

Lord Hastings bent his head and looked down at her. With her lips parted just so, she looked temptingly kissable. But he thrust the thought aside. An alarm had sounded in his brain; indeed, he could hear the chains of leg-shackles clanking noisily, as if from a deep, cavernous dungeon! To kiss a respectable woman like Felicity Bell was tantamount to a betrothal. And, the Lord knows, he had no desire to be betrothed to anyone.

Besides, Felicity Bell was the last woman in the world for *him!* If he ever got about to marriage, he'd much rather have a biddable lass. Not some hard-headed, managing female like this one!

Eager to dispatch with his reason for bringing her outside, but not yet far enough away from the castle to suit him, Lord Hastings forced himself to be conversational. "We walk, Miss Bell, in the time 'twixt the gloaming and the mirk.' "

"How Scottish you sound!" she remarked, those large green orbs turned confidingly to his face. How charming she was when she took a notion to be charming, thought the earl. But he hardened himself against her charm and determinedly walked her farther into the woods. Presently the forest opened to a wide meadow and a still, small loch surrounded by fir trees.

"Well, I must say I'm relieved to discover the loch to be of such moderate proportions," said Felicity, arching a brow at him.

"Why so, Miss Bell?" the earl asked, intrigued despite himself.

"Because no beastie could possibly fit its ponderous body in there!" she stated firmly, daring him to cavil with her.

"Perhaps it's a spawning pond for the beast's eggs," Lord Hastings could not resist suggesting. "The loch is close to the firth. And, since we were privy to Sally's riveting tale, we know beasties travel on solid ground when necessary."

"You are the outside of enough!" exclaimed Felicity, removing her arm from the snug crook of his elbow and stepping back. She glared at him and ran her hands up and down her arms as if she'd caught a sudden chill.

Ah, good! She was perturbed with him. Now that they were on their usual footing, the earl felt a deal more comfortable. He could commence with the lecture.

"Miss Bell," he began in a firm voice, "I am having serious reservations about bringing you to Culzean."

"Indeed! Why is that, Lord Hastings?" Felicity's confiding manner had disappeared entirely. Her tone was haughty and offended.

"You knew I was unwilling at the beginning to assist you in your pursuit of the eloping couple, didn't you? But I felt it my duty to lend you protection, since you showed about as much common sense as your average Johnny Raw! A defenceless, unescorted female jauntering about the countryside! And in a gig, no less! It boggles the brain!"

"I explained why I was travelling alone," defended Felicity. "And you know why I was in such a great hurry and took a notion to borrow a gig! But I did not, as well you know! Why are you bringing all this up again?"

Lord Hastings endeavoured to calm himself. For some reason, the idea of Felicity's reckless behaviour rankled him now more than ever.

Ignoring her question, he continued, "Then, at Gretna Green, though I deplored your methods, I began to think perhaps it wouldn't be such a bad thing if you came to Culzean and lent your sister a little moral support. I know how Grandfather can be, and you told me that Susan was a trifle timid, but..." He paused. Felicity was eyeing him impatiently. He forged ahead. "I know you mean well,

Miss Bell, but I think you carry this burning desire to protect your sister rather too far.''

"What do you mean, Lord Hastings?'' The calm manner in which she asked the question seemed more ominous than if she'd screamed at him. She folded her arms across her chest and waited for his answer.

Lord Hastings stooped to pick up a flat rock and skip it across the peat-thick loch, shimmering emerald in the twilight. He was biding time. He must choose his words carefully.

Felicity watched his manoeuvrings and commented dryly, "Four skips. Very good. Now could you please continue?''

"It is difficult to explain, Miss Bell, but somehow I think your sister would do better if you, well...left her to her own devices.''

"I still don't understand.'' Felicity waited. The look in her eyes bordered on the murderous.

"Well, then, if you want an example... That picture of the Highlander troops was Susan's, wasn't it? Had you not interfered, Grandfather would have known that even timid little Susan had a taste for the humorous.''

"How unfair you are!'' cried Felicity, stamping her foot, her fists resting on her shapely hips. "I admit I made a stupid blunder. But I'm not usually so inept. You must give me a little credit!''

"Oh, I do, I do!'' he was quick to qualify. "In fact you are so *very* capable you quite overshadow your younger sister, giving her no recourse but to leave everything up to you! Perhaps if you allowed her to handle her own affairs, she'd acquire a little confidence! Now that she is practically a married woman, perhaps Susan wishes to live her own life, Miss Bell!'' There, he'd said it. Actually, he'd said rather more than he'd intended.

It was obvious to Lord Hastings that Felicity was waging an inner battle. She probably wanted to call him every kind of scoundrel, but her gentlewoman's upbringing demanded that she refrain from such vulgarity. Her eyes glittered angrily, her full, rosy lips were tightly compressed and her breath came quick and shallow.

Against his will, his eyes drifted to the front of her bodice. The thin material of her gown expanded across her breasts with every intake of offended breath she took. Such passion! What an armful of delight she would be in his bed! But that was never to be, alas.

When his eyes returned to her face, she was even angrier, if that were possible!

''How dare you look at me as if I were a . . . a . . .'' Her eyes blinked with the effort of coming up with a suitable metaphor. ''A bowl of fruit!''

Lord Hastings let loose a bark of laughter. ''How clever of you, Miss Bell! You couldn't have come up with a better comparison!''

''Don't patronize me, Lord Hastings!'' she warned him. ''Oh, you make me so *very* angry! You barely know me, or my sister! How dare you presume to lecture me about my relationship with Susan? How dare you suggest I am a...a meddlesome old woman?''

''I did *not* say that!'' insisted the earl, stunned by the unfortunate meaning she'd gleaned from his words.

''I was distressed by something Susan had just told me when you came into the drawingroom this evening. Fool that I am, I thought you suggested this walk to perhaps lend a listening ear and...and... Oh, never mind!'' Felicity abruptly turned her back on Lord Hastings and walked several feet away.

Lord Hastings sighed deeply. *Now what's to do?* he wondered. He had noticed her agitation when he'd entered the drawingroom, and wondered about the cause of her distress. He had even felt a moment's gratification when her eyes had immediately sought his. But he'd been so caught up in his own purpose, so determined to advise her about Susan that he'd quite forgotten everything else.

He moved to stand just behind her. He lifted his hands to rest them comfortingly, apologetically on her shoulders. Suddenly he thought better of such a gesture. He did not trust himself to touch her. He hastily stuffed his hands in the pockets of his inexpressibles, where they would behave themselves.

''Why don't we go inside, Miss Bell?'' he suggested. ''You must be very tired from your journey.''

"Indeed I am" was her stiff reply. Then she made a neat turn and marched ahead to the castle without once looking at him.

Not to be accused of ungentlemanly behaviour, Lord Hastings caught her up. After a brief, non-speaking tug of war, he secured her arm against his side and politely escorted the unwilling damsel to the castle doors.

CHAPTER SIX

THE NEXT DAY, Felicity and Susan were shut up all morning with the local seamstress. Gowns for the wedding festivities had to be made up with all due haste, and there was not time enough to solicit the services of a fashionable modiste from one of the large towns. But after a few minutes' consultation with the seamstress, Felicity was convinced that the nimble-fingered woman, and the two daughters who assisted her, knew exactly what to do.

In fact, besides a dress for the wedding, Felicity ordered another dress to be made up and one of Susan's riding habits to be altered to fit her. Lieutenant Kennedy had said that they would assuredly go riding one fine day before the wedding, and Felicity did not wish to be left out of such a delightful scheme.

For the wedding Susan would be dressed in white, but with a tartan sash draped from one shoulder across her bodice and fastened at the side. Susan would be beautiful on her wedding day. Felicity thought it a shame that her family would not be able to see her looking so well. But then to wish for Henry and his brood, and Aunt Mathilda, was to invite trouble. By now, she wished for nothing more than for Susan to be safely married to Kyle.

Felicity indulged her usual fancy for bright colours and chose a jonquil silk to be made up in simple Grecian lines. The colour was as clear and true as a dew-sparkled daffodil. Holding the swath of material against her cheek and gazing into the mirror, Felicity wished she felt as lively as she looked.

Last night she'd lain awake, pondering Lord Hastings's advice concerning Susan. At first Felicity refused to give his words any consideration, dismissing them out-of-hand as the blusterings of an arrogant man.

But after a time, she began to wonder if Susan did feel a little resentful of her appearance at the castle. She wondered if Susan felt as smothered by Felicity's well-meaning solicitude as she was by Henry's constant strictures. And what if Felicity *had* thwarted Susan's confidence by forever interfering and solving her sister's problems for her?

"Felicity, Kyle means to take me for a ride this afternoon. Won't you come along?"

Felicity looked down into her sister's beaming face. Her expression did not suggest the agony of resentment and thwarted confidence! Lord Hastings *must* be wrong!

"I'd love to join you, Susan," Felicity promptly replied with a smile. "I'm anxious to see more of this beautiful country. Though, I daresay, you will become familiar with every hillock and moor as the years go by!''

Susan smiled her approval of such an agreeable idea, then said, ''I know! Why don't we take along some food and have a nuncheon out-of-doors!''

''Just the thing, sister!'' approved Felicity. ''Run along and find Kyle, so that he might order us a basket of food from the kitchen. I'll just go to my room and freshen up a bit.''

Susan skipped away to find her beloved and Felicity returned to her bedchamber. Today she wore her blue gown, and since she was already dressed, she had nothing to do to ready herself for the outing besides smooth her face with a little Bloom of Ninon. She had a most troublesome propensity to freckle and she was hoping the lotion would shield her somewhat from the sun's rays.

Her hair was twisted and braided in a rather classical style by the talented chambermaid and Felicity was tempted to dispense with a bonnet, but she remembered her complexion and dutifully covered up the gleaming copper tresses.

A half an hour later, Felicity met Susan in the hall and they descended the stairs together. ''Did the lieutenant say whether we are taking an open carriage, Susan? It's such a beautiful day, it would be delightful to have the sky as our roof!''

''We're going in a gig,'' answered Susan, pulling on a pair of neat kid gloves to match her rose-coloured gown.

"A gig!" exclaimed Felicity. "What a sad crush with the three of us! Then there is the basket to consider, too. Hadn't we ought to take a carriage?"

They had reached the foyer and as the footman opened the front doors, Susan said, "Don't be silly, Felicity! There will be four of us and we're taking *two* gigs."

They'd stepped outside into the sunny front courtyard, and just as Susan said, there were two gigs waiting to be boarded. Kyle stood at the front gig, stroking the long nose of a chestnut horse and Lord Hastings stood at the other, conversing with his grandfather.

How stupid not to have realized that *he* would come along, thought Felicity. And travelling thusly in separate carriages, she was doomed to spend an entire afternoon tête-à-tête with the earl. Dared she feign a sudden onset of the headache? She was considering this course of action when the earl caught sight of her and smiled his devilish smile. There was a challenge in his black eyes, and Felicity was loath to stand down from a challenge.

Susan had already joined Kyle, luckily only stubbing her toe against a slightly raised cobblestone in the process. Felicity hung back, afraid to go, yet unwilling to cry craven. When Lord Ailsa looked round and stared questioningly at her, her decision was made.

Indeed, there really was nothing to be afraid of, was there? If Lord Hastings took it into his head to lecture her, or tease her, or, worst of all, *flirt* with her, she'd simply ignore him, just as she'd done at breakfast. She took a deep breath, squared her shoulders and stepped forward.

"Bonny day for a jaunt in the country, eh, Miss Bell?" Lord Ailsa said.

"Yes, very lovely, my lord!" she replied graciously, favouring the old gentleman with a radiant smile.

Lord Hastings extended his hand to assist her into the carriage and while she was compelled to allow this common courtesy, she refused to look at him.

After Lord Hastings had gone round the gig and pulled himself easily up and onto the narrow seat beside her, Lord Ailsa remarked, "I suppose ye'll be back fer tea, then?"

"Oh, much sooner than that, my—" Felicity began, but Lord Hastings interrupted.

"Perhaps we will, or perhaps not," he said. "You had better not look for us till dinner."

"We're going so far as that?" blurted Felicity, goaded into speaking to the earl.

"I haven't the slightest idea where we're going," said the earl with a lazy smile. "Kyle leads the way. He knows the countryside much better than I do."

"But I should have thought we'd fix on a particular destination, not just drive aimlessly about!"

"Where's your taste for adventure?" Lord Hastings chided. "Besides, after all the vast country we've crossed together, Miss Bell, what's another few miles?''

Lord Ailsa laughed. "Och, he's got ye there, lass!''

Felicity snapped open her parasol. "That was another situation altogether, as well you know!'' she informed them with a show of affronted dignity. "Good day, Lord Ailsa!''

"Good day, lass,'' said Lord Ailsa, still chuckling. Then they were off.

Felicity stared stonily ahead as they left the courtyard. They headed north through an open stretch of moor. Far to the right were woods. To the left the heather abruptly gave way to steep cliffs that overlooked the pebbled sand below and the Firth of Clyde. Felicity longed to drink in the lovely view of the sea, but she would have had to turn her head towards the earl to do so.

"It will be a deucedly long afternoon if you persist in giving me the cut, Miss Bell. Why don't you call me an impertinent jackanapes and have done with it! Then, perhaps you won't get a stiff neck endeavouring to ignore me!''

Felicity turned her head slightly, though she still refused to look him in the eye. "Then you admit you were impertinent last evening?''

"Well,'' Lord Hastings demurred, "I will admit that I was putting in my oar where it wasn't wanted. That is, I offered an unsolicited opinion, which is much like meddling. And since I was, in essence, accusing you of meddling, it was a bit hypocritical of me.''

"Good heavens, Lord Hastings! Can it be? Are you apologizing?'' Felicity feigned shock and turned wide eyes to the earl.

"Don't get sassy, lass,'' he warned with a grudging, lopsided smile. "I was goaded into the error. 'Tis deuced difficult standing by whilst someone makes a mull of things!''

Felicity stiffened and returned her gaze to the less irritating and therefore more pleasing view of the horse's tail. "That was a backhanded apology if ever I heard one! Do please spare me further penitence!''

Lord Hastings laughed the laugh he had obviously inherited from his grandfather, along with his looks. It was so pleasant a sound that Felicity began to wish she could forget her pride and anger and be comfortable.

"Why don't we set aside our differences for now, Miss Bell?'' Lord Hastings soon suggested, uncannily voicing her very thoughts. "It's such a lovely day and I want to be comfortable, don't you?''

Felicity wanted very much to be comfortable. But while they might cease to quarrel with each other, there was still the unsettling closeness of his powerful thigh touching hers. And one must not discount the scent of him, either. It was so clean, yet masculine. Then, too, there was the sight of his lean fingers holding the ribbons. His handling of the horse suggested strength tempered by gentleness. Good heavens, how could she ever truly be comfortable in the company of such a man? He managed to discompose her by his mere proximity!

"Well, Miss Bell? What shall it be? A truce, or all-out war?"

Felicity turned to look at Lord Hastings and felt surrender seeping into her bones. She was ill equipped for battle this day. She had much better agree to a truce.

"I don't wish to fight with you," she admitted. "But the terms of truce require that you do not lecture me about Susan. Can you agree to those terms?"

"Yes, Miss Bell," said the earl with a disarming smile. "I can and I will refrain from lecturing you...today."

Felicity did not like the way he had won the upper hand once again, but she decided to be satisfied for "today" and settled back into her seat with more ease. But she'd been so engrossed in peace negotiations with the earl that she hadn't realized how far ahead Susan and Kyle were.

"Goodness, we must be plodding along! Look where Susan and Kyle are!"

"We are moving at a good clip, Miss Bell," Lord Hastings returned calmly. "Susan and Kyle are trotting along at a speed the horse could not possibly sustain all day. Kyle probably wishes to put a little distance between us to secure a bit of privacy."

Felicity remembered her suspicions from the previous night and said, "I daresay they've had quite enough privacy already for an unmarried couple!"

"There is never enough privacy for lovers," said the earl.

"Yes, but if it leads to—" Felicity cut herself off. Lord Hastings had agreed not to lecture her about Susan, but she did not wish to tempt him by bringing up the subject. Besides, she ought not to discuss such a topic as pre-marriage intimacies with Lord Hastings. What was she thinking? But lately her words tumbled out without benefit of thought.

Lord Hastings wisely did not request that she finish her sentence, though he gave her a searching look. They fell into a rather languid mood of camaraderie. The sun beat down on Felicity's parasol, enveloping her in a warm haze of contentment. The clop-clop of the horse's hooves lulled her nearly to sleep, but the scenery and Lord Hastings's occasional wicked remark kept her sufficiently entertained and alarmed to stay awake.

After a time, he said offhandedly, "Since we've called a truce, would you like to tell me what was troubling you last night?"

Felicity shook her head. "No. But I thank you for asking." Lord Hastings inclined his head and let the subject drop. While she had decided that it was not a matter she could discuss with the earl, Felicity was still pleased that he'd offered to listen.

They were passing through a thicket of trees along a winding, narrow lane when Lord Hastings suddenly exclaimed, "Good God, I'm hungry!"

"Yes, no doubt you are," Felicity observed dryly. "It must be at least an hour since last you ate."

"That long? Thank goodness I brought something with me!"

The earl reached into his jacket pocket and produced a large orange. "A beauty, ain't she?" he said. "Grandfather's orangery grows the best oranges this side of Spain!"

"But how will you peel it?" asked Felicity. "Or do you eat them peel and all?"

"I'm not a beastie, Miss Bell. I have *some* civilized habits! Will you peel it for me?"

"I had much rather take the ribbons. I'm a crackwhip, you know. Comes of driving my own horses in Yorkshire all the time."

"Naturally," said the earl, frowning. But still he held the orange and the ribbons, and appeared to be debating Felicity's suggestion.

"Oh, never say you do not trust me!" admonished Felicity. "Or are you one of those men who don't think women ought to hold the ribbons? Rather an antiquated idea!"

"It's not that," he said testily. "It's just that this is a rather narrow road which is difficult to manoeuvre."

"Remember, you said yourself I am a very capable woman!"

"Yes, so I did." He looked longingly at the orange. "Very well. Take the ribbons."

He handed Felicity the ribbons and watched closely while she demonstrated her skill. Since she tooled the horses along without the slightest change of rhythm, the earl relaxed and peeled his orange, tossing the rinds in the passing shrubberies.

As Lord Hastings popped the last orange section into his mouth, they emerged from the thicket and were presented with a fork in the road. Kyle and Susan had been out of sight since they'd entered the thicket. Without slowing the horse or consulting the earl, Felicity took the road headed west.

"Dash it, Miss Bell! Where do you think you're going?" Lord Hastings asked.

"Well, since we don't know which road they took, I took the road which most appealed to me!" she explained.

"Oh, that smacks of sound reasoning, doesn't it?" he observed sarcastically. "Give me the ribbons. We've got to make a narrow turn here."

"Why are you so sure they took the other road?" argued Felicity.

"Because this one gets ugly! Now, do give me the ribbons, Miss Bell!"

Felicity was about to inform him that a narrow turn was not beyond her powers of execution, when they hit a huge hole in the road. Besides the jolt which suspended them above their seats a good twelve inches, the carriage lurched to the side and threw them abruptly to the ground.

After the initial shock of flying through the air and landing hard on her back, Felicity was privy to a show of fireworks not unlike the displays at Vauxhall. Lights spiraled against a black background and burst into stars of various shapes and colours. When the darkness finally receded and the stars gave way to the light of a bright midday sun, Felicity was made suddenly aware of a thundering headache.

"Felicity! Good God, lass, are ye all right?"

Felicity blinked several times and Lord Hastings came into view. He was kneeling beside her. But he did not sound his usual self. She was sure of it; a definite Scottish burr laced his speech. And he didn't look his usual self, either. He seemed beside himself with worry, not to mention the disarranged neckcloth dusted with dirt, the large rent in his jacket-sleeve and the scrape on his forehead, oozing blood.

And it was all her fault! Felicity struggled to sit up.

"Lie still, lass!" growled the earl. "We dinna know the extent of yer injuries!"

"I'm quite all right, other than this blasted headache," Felicity assured him.

"Ye'll lie still till I tell ye otherwise!" Lord Hastings commanded.

Felicity lay still while the earl proceeded to examine her for injuries. Under any other circumstances, Lord Hastings's actions would be extremely improper. He slid his hands up and under each arm and leg, flexing the joints gently. He lifted Felicity's head, cradled her neck and instructed her to turn this way and that. Lastly, he gingerly probed the back of her head.

"Ouch!" cried Felicity.

"Aye, you've got a goose-egg the size of a billiard ball," he informed her. "It appears to be the worst of your injuries. You're going to have the devil of a headache and be stiff and sore for several hours, but you'll live!" At the end of this pronouncement, Lord Hastings heaved a relieved sigh. As his concern decreased, the Scottish intonation of his words seemed to lessen proportionately.

"Now may I sit up?" Felicity demanded.

"Aye... Yes, if you feel up to it. Here, lean against this tree stump."

Felicity sat up and obediently scooted over to a nearby tree stump. Thank God she hadn't landed on *that!* The heather was knee-high and Felicity supposed that it had cushioned their fall somewhat.

"Are you all right?" she asked him, now that her wits were restored. "Your head—"

"'Tis nothing but a flea bite," Lord Hastings scoffed. "Sit still. I must see to the horse."

Felicity watched the earl walk briskly away to calm the horse. Lord Hastings certainly did not appear the least injured. Thank goodness for that! But the frightened horse stamped and pulled frantically against its traces, and the gig lay on its side, the top wheel still spinning. What a shocking mull she'd

made of things! And all because she must prove to
the earl that she was as capable as he was to execute
a neat turn in the road! Oh, her abominable pride
and stubbornness!

Lord Hastings soothed the horse and led it to a
nearby tree, tethering it to a low-hanging branch.
Then he returned to where Felicity sat and stooped
down beside her. Felicity averted her eyes. She was
ashamed to look at him.

"How are you feeling?" he asked.

Felicity risked a quick glance at him and blanched
at the sincere concern reflected in his eyes.

"I'm feeling like a complete dolt! Why don't you
rant or rave or...something! This is all my fault, you
know!"

"I know," he sighed, lowering himself to sit beside her.

"Then why are you being so kind?"

Lord Hastings reached inside his coat pocket and
extracted a snowy white handkerchief. He pressed it
against his bleeding forehead. "I thought I'd let you
recover from your injuries before I killed you. So
much more sporting, don't you know?"

Felicity choked on a laugh. "How can you be droll
at a time like this?"

"Really, Miss Bell, had you rather I ranted and
raved?" he asked her, his black eyes a vivid contrast
to the handkerchief skimming his brows.

"No, it should only make my head ache all the
worse," she admitted. "What shall we do? Do you

think Kyle and Susan will discover we're missing and return for us?''

''When they stop to eat, perhaps then they'll wonder where we are, but not before! Kyle is not likely to keep his usual wits about him in his besotted condition. He has eyes for Susan only.'' Lord Hastings grimaced as if a sudden, unfortunate thought just occurred to him. ''Dash it all,'' he said, ''*they* have the picnic basket!''

It was quite obvious to Felicity that in Lord Hastings's estimation, this was the worst of the debacle. A gash on the forehead was nothing compared to an empty stomach.

''Well, the two of us can right the gig,'' she suggested. ''I assure you, I'm quite ready and able to travel.''

''Righting the carriage is not the problem! *I* could easily do that myself!'' he informed her. ''The right wheel is damaged beyond repair.''

''Couldn't we ride the horse back to Culzean?''

''We could,'' he grimly acknowledged. ''But it would likely kill the beast. I am not exactly a lightweight, you know. I must always choose large, muscular horses to withstand my size. And with the two of us riding...''

''I see your point,'' said Felicity, frowning. ''Then perhaps we ought to start walking and maybe someone will come along and take us up in their carriage.''

"Which is exactly my plan," said the earl. "With one exception. I shall walk, but you shall ride the horse."

"Oh, you beastie!" cried Felicity. "You know very well my conscience will make me miserable if I am allowed the comfort of riding while you trudge alongside! It's my fault we're in this muddle in the first place. I won't ride!"

The earl smiled grimly. "Yes, you will! I must extract vengeance somehow. Come along, Miss Bell. For once in your life, be obedient!"

Lord Hastings stood up, stuffed his bloodied handkerchief into a trousers' pocket, and pulled Felicity to her feet. Then he stooped and slid his hands under her arms and legs, lifting her.

"I won't do it, I tell you!" cried Felicity, squirming frantically in his viselike embrace. He walked unsteadily to the horse, her wildly flinging legs throwing them off balance.

"Yes, you will!" he insisted, dropping her legs to the ground, but still supporting her with an arm round her shoulders. Then, turning her to face him, Lord Hastings placed his large hands about her waist to lift her onto the horse's back. Suddenly Felicity felt dizzy and she swayed against the earl's broad chest.

"Oh, dear," she moaned, clutching his neckcloth in an attempt to keep herself in an upright position. But while the world around Felicity tilted and spun in dizzying circles, she became aware of the one steadying influence—Lord Hastings, his firm hands on her waist and the solid comfort of his warm chest.

Felicity's senses were swimming, and she no longer knew whether she was light-headed from her injury or from her close proximity to the earl. But the broad chest beckoned, and her hands slipped away from their grip on his lordship's bedraggled neckcloth and lay, palms down, against his waistcoat. Even through the several layers of material, she could feel his heart beating hard and fast.

Confused, she lifted her eyes to his. This did not prove to be a wise decision. His black eyes flashed with strongly felt emotion. There were beads of perspiration on his upper lip, and Felicity found herself intrigued with looking at them. His warm breath fanned her face. . . .

Abruptly the earl tensed. "Is that a carriage I hear?"

Felicity listened, too. Yes, someone was coming. She pulled herself away from the earl and turned round, leaning against the horse's flanks for support.

"Good God! What's happened here?"

It was Kyle and Susan. Obviously Lord Hastings had underestimated his besotted cousin's ability to keep his wits about him. Help was at hand, thought Felicity dully. Then why was she so disappointed?

"WHAT A RECALCITRANT invalid you are!" scolded Susan. "If you won't stay in your bedchamber and

rest, you ought at least to recline on the sofa. Sitting
up thusly cannot be good for your headache. And I
daresay you would do well to stay in your bedchamber to avoid the noise down here we have to make to
get Geddes's attention, and then be subject to his ear-
shattering replies!"

Felicity answered in a firm voice, "If I wanted to
recline, I'd have stayed abed, Susan. And a few loud
voices would be most welcome. I refuse to mope
about as if I were soliciting sympathy!"

"No, that is not your way. But surely you ought to
lie down or *something*..."

"Hush, Susan. They're coming!"

"They" were Kyle, Lord Ailsa and Lord Hastings, just risen from their after-dinner potations.
Susan stumbled over to a chair and sat down before
Lord Ailsa's piercing gaze could send her sprawling
to the floor. Felicity had not joined the gentlemen for
dinner, so her presence in the drawingroom caused
somewhat of a stir.

"Miss Bell!" exclaimed Kyle. "What are ye doing out of your chamber?"

"Lass, had ye ought t'be about so soon?" questioned Lord Ailsa, bending to claim her hand and
chafe it between his two.

Felicity darted a glance at Lord Hastings. He was
scowling at her. The wound on his forehead had been
thoroughly cleansed and attended to and looked
much better. A flood of warmth crept through Felicity as she remembered the way he'd held her in his

arms earlier that day. That he'd been compelled to do so to keep her from falling she conveniently forgot. It was a strangely exciting, frightening experience, unlike any she'd felt before.

"Please don't fuss over me," Felicity begged, laughing lightly. "I'm quite all right! And, if you must know, I would have been happy to stay in my room all evening to please you all, but something's happened—"

"What's happened?" demanded Lord Hastings, stepping forward. "Did you faint?"

"No, no, nothing of the sort," Felicity hastily assured him, flustered by his concern. "It just occurred to me that Hugo, my coachman, hasn't arrived. He's had plenty of time to get here from Gretna Green and I left word that he should join me here immediately upon receiving the note."

"Could he have got lost?" Lord Ailsa asked.

"I don't think so. Lord Hastings gave me specific instructions on how to get here, which I faithfully repeated in my note to Hugo. He's not the least dull-witted. I begin to fear he's either encountered some sort of trouble on the way, or did not receive the note!"

"Egad," growled Lord Hastings. "I suppose you know what *that* means?"

"Yes," sighed Felicity. "If he didn't receive the note, due, no doubt, to the fumblings of the pistol-waving innkeeper at Gretna, he won't know what's become of me and will race back to Yorkshire with news of my abduction. Panic will reign supreme, Aunt Mathilda will fall into the throes of a violent spasm and Henry will be summoned from London to defend my honour! It boggles the brain, doesn't it?''

"We ought'na to leap to conclusions!" Lord Ailsa scolded. "Perhaps the coachman is merely delayed. Ye sent yer brother and yer aunt a letter, dinna ye?"

"Yes, but if Hugo returned to Yorkshire he is sure to have got there before my letters ever reached their destination. Once Aunt Mathilda's flown into a pelter, she will stop at nothing to locate me. Suppose she doesn't wait for Henry and hires her own post-chaise to come after me?"

"But she does'na even know the first place to look, Miss Bell," reasoned Kyle. "She'll fret and flutter for a time, to be sure. But once she's received yer letter, she'll calm down."

"I suppose you're right," said Felicity doubtfully.

"There's really nothing else you can do just now, Miss Bell. Don't let it trouble you," advised the earl. "We must simply wait and see what will happen in the next few days."

Yes, thought Felicity, *what* will *happen in the next few days?* If she could judge by the way Lord Hastings worded his sentence, he intended to be included in all the excitement. But she supposed it was reasonable that he would wish to stay for Kyle's wedding. Though unfortunately her own peace of mind would be seriously jeopardized by the earl's presence at the castle. As much as she would wish to deny it, mayhap an old spinster like herself had as little defence against a pair of black Gypsy eyes as any green girl, which was a lowering thought, indeed.

"Miss Bell, why don't you take some laudanum?" Lord Hastings suggested in a coaxing voice. "You require rest and it will help you sleep."

"Absolutely not," Felicity said. "I refuse to quack myself!" But judging by his lordship's determined expression, Felicity knew she would not escape without an argument.

CHAPTER SEVEN

WHEN FELICITY ENTERED the breakfast room the next morning, she found everyone already assembled and in various stages of breakfasting. Owing to the small dose of opiate she was coaxed to take the night before, she'd lain in bed rather longer than usual. And a slight grogginess had plagued her throughout her bath, but finally disappeared when the chambermaid had vigorously brushed her hair. Now she felt quite well, her headache was gone and her limbs were only a trifle stiff.

Upon her entrance, the three gentlemen stood. While she knew their interest was quite well meaning, it was rather unsettling to be the object of their combined scrutiny. Three pairs of piercing dark eyes seemed to take in every detail of her person, though it was the blackest pair of eyes which disturbed her the most.

"Good morning!" she said gaily, endeavouring to put their minds at ease about her slight injuries. Felicity sat next to Susan and smiled at Lord Ailsa.

"Och, ye must be feeling much better, lass!" said Lord Ailsa with a satisfied nod of his head.

"Much better! Do sit down, my lord. The three of you standing about, like so many grim giants, quite overwhelms me!"

The gentlemen obediently sat, and Lord Ailsa returned to reading his newspaper, while Felicity accepted some tea and toast from one of the servants.

"You had ought to eat more than that," advised Lord Hastings, frowning at her Spartan breakfast. "There's eggs and potatoes, kippers and ham at the sideboard."

Felicity felt a prick of irritation. The way Lord Hastings was admonishing her to eat seemed to show an interest in her welfare generally held to be the right of only a close relative, rather like a brother...or a husband.

Last evening, when he'd practically forced her to take the laudanum, she'd been too weak and ill to engage in a battle of wills. But while she had the strength to resist, she'd not be bullied!

"Never fear, Lord Hastings, I shall not faint away for lack of sustenance," she assured him in a sweet voice, but with a quelling look. "I'm quite used to taking care of myself. I have done so for many years."

While the earl raised a brow at Felicity's pert retort, Kyle laughed. "Jamie, Felicity, er, Miss Bell is a might smaller than us. She does'na need to eat the way we do!"

"Do call me Felicity, Lieutenant, if it comes more naturally to your lips," Felicity suggested, smiling. "After all, we *will* be brother and sister!"

"And might *I* call you Felicity?" Lord Hastings enquired with a mischievous glint in his eyes. "After all, *we* will be cousins!"

Felicity found herself at a loss for words. How could she refuse him without seeming rude?

"Yes!" cried Susan. "What a capital idea! We must all be comfortable and call one another by our Christian names!" But when Susan discovered that her impulsive outburst had drawn Lord Ailsa's attention away from the newspaper, she stammered, "Th-that is, of course, excepting Lord Ailsa. At his age...rather I mean, er, he is much too, er, stately to called by his Chr-Christian name!"

Felicity watched Susan agonize through this bumbling speech with a sinking sensation. Susan could just not seem to overcome her fear of the marquess! "Lord Ailsa, what Susan means is that your dignity and station in life warrant a more respectful address—"

"I rather think Grandfather knows what Susan means," put in the earl with a speaking look at Felicity, who immediately bristled. "Or else if he is unclear of her meaning, I'm sure he could ask for further explanation, at which time Susan might oblige him!"

"I find it demmed uncivil for the lot of ye to be discussing me in my presence, as if I were a wee bairn!" barked Lord Ailsa with a thunderous scowl.

"I beg pardon, Grandfather," Lord Hastings said soothingly, and added, "How do your plans for the party progress?"

Lord Ailsa eyed his grandson. "I'm not a doddering fool yet, Jamie. I know ye're trying to distract me."

"Then mayhap we should talk about something else," suggested Kyle hurriedly. "Felicity, what say ye to another outing?"

"What? Another carriage ride?" she exclaimed a little nervously. She had no desire to be tête-à-tête with the earl again.

"Nay. Jamie and I were talking this morning and thought it might be amusing to show ye ladies one of our childhood haunts. It's within easy walking distance. I dinna think it will tax yer strength in the least!"

"What childhood haunt is this?" enquired Felicity, still sceptical.

"We'll not tell ye just yet," said Kyle, an impish gleam in his eyes making him look quite boyish.

"I'd much rather know where we're going before I agree to such a scheme," Felicity demurred.

"Again I ask, where's your spirit of adventure, Felicity?" enquired the earl, stressing his use of her Christian name. Felicity knew it for a double hit. Firstly, he was suggesting that if she didn't go, she was a dull-stick. Secondly, he'd used her Christian name when she'd not specifically allowed him the privilege.

Felicity was about to allude to yesterday's carriage accident. She was about to suggest that perhaps her "spirit" had been broken along with the carriage wheel until she remembered that the entire thing had been her fault, yet the earl had never once rebuked her. And then there was the gentle way he'd checked her for injuries. She'd been right about his hands. Despite their size and strength, they could be gentle. Very gentle, indeed.

"Well, Felicity, what say ye?" prompted Kyle.

It was obvious by Susan's expression that she wished very much to see Kyle's childhood haunt. Felicity was ashamed of her mulishness. After all, it was the very trait which had got her into the devil of a fix yesterday.

"It sounds delightful, Kyle," said Felicity at last. "When shall we go?"

"Splendid! We shall go directly after we've finished eating our breakfast!" was Kyle's enthusiastic response. "We'll return in time for nuncheon."

"Thank God," murmured Lord Hastings.

"Aye. Ye had best go while the tide's well out," advised Lord Ailsa. "There's a new moon, Kyle, and when there's a new moon the tides come in with a vengeance."

"Hush, Grandfather, or else ye'll give us away," admonished Kyle.

Lord Ailsa snorted, and returned to his paper. Felicity pondered on this clue as to where they were going, and could imagine nothing reasonable. Since they weren't taking a nuncheon, she didn't think the island of Arran was their destination.

"Don't cudgel your brain too strenuously, Miss Bell," teased Lord Hastings, rising and pushing his chair neatly against the table. "Mayhap the effort will bring on the headache again, and you wouldn't wish to miss our outing, now would you?"

"Bring warm shawls, ladies," said Kyle, rising from the table also. "And wear sturdy shoes. Shall we meet in, say, half an hour in the entrance hall? Till then, lass." He stooped to give Susan a brief kiss on the crown of her head, smiled warmly down at her and left the room.

Against her will, Felicity's eyes slid over to where Lord Hastings still stood, his lean, brown hands loosely circling the ornate carvings at the top of his chair. He had returned to calling her "Miss Bell." Did he do so out of respect, or was he simply trying to vex her?

"Till then, lass," he said, repeating Kyle's endearment. Then he winked and left the room. Felicity blushed. But at least he hadn't kissed her!

THE FOOTPATH DOWN from the cliff had been gradual and easy. But now that they walked along the sands, more exertion was required. Susan walked just ahead of Kyle, and Felicity had naturally been coupled again with Lord Hastings. She was polite but aloof. To engage in much conversation with Lord Hastings always seemed to lead to vexation. The late morning sun beat down on them, and despite the sea breeze, Felicity was growing rather warm.

"I don't understand why Kyle advised us to bring shawls," complained Felicity, clutching her parasol. "'Tis hot enough without them!"

"You will presently understand," Lord Hastings said.

"Where could we possibly be going?" persisted Felicity, goaded into speech after another few minutes of trudging through the sand. "It is a bright, warm day, yet you carry a lantern and Kyle totes a blanket! I confess myself utterly mystified!" Lord Hastings did not reply. Felicity clicked her tongue in exasperation and shook her head. She was at the mercy of these hard-headed Scotsmen and simply had to wait.

The high cliffs which overlooked the sands gradually diminished in height and curved to meet the sea. If they walked much longer they'd run smack up against a wall of granite.

"Over there, you see?" Lord Hastings cupped Felicity's elbow and turned her slightly, pointing with his other hand.

Felicity looked, then exclaimed, "Why it's a cave!"

Near where the cliff met the sea was an entrance about seven feet high and just as wide. Smooth, sea-honed boulders of every size were scattered all about in front of it, as if by a playful giant. Seagulls preened and squawked a greeting from their rocky perches.

Now Kyle led the way across a pebbly expanse of beach, veering around circles of bubbling sand, tide pools percolating with tiny sea creatures, and swirls of glistening seaweed left by the ebb tide. Here and there lay driftwood, thickly encrusted with barnacles, their leafless, writhing fingers reaching skyward. Obviously at flood tide the mouth of the cave was inaccessible except by boat.

"Oh, Felicity, isn't this exciting!" squealed Susan, turning round just long enough to share a wide smile with her sister. Then she linked her arm with Kyle's and strode eagerly ahead.

It *was* rather exciting. Felicity had never been inside a cave before. The thrill of adventure infused her, and she no longer felt the least bit weary or hot. She even forgot to be irritated with Lord Hastings.

Now they had reached the mouth of the cave and stepped just inside. The cool air was heavy with moisture and the tang of salt. The utter darkness was slightly relieved by thin shafts of light filtering through tiny cracks in the ceiling, but still Felicity could not see the opposite end of the cave. The trickle of water echoed and magnified through the cool, deep dark.

"Enchanting!" breathed Felicity. "A pirates' den!"

"Aye, that and whatever else our lively imaginations chose to make of it," said Kyle.

"My favourite was the beastie's lair," murmured Lord Hastings.

Felicity's eyes snapped to the earl's face, but he was looking round the cave with an arrested expression.

"Ye were always the beastie," remembered Kyle, with a nostalgic smile. "And I was Saint Columba, calling forth the power of God to smite ye down!"

"As I recall, you were rather more apt to use your dirk to smite the beastie," said the earl with an affectionate grin. "Usually a blunt piece of driftwood, wasn't it?"

"Aye," laughed Kyle.

"Can we go farther in?" asked Susan, fairly dancing with excitement. Felicity marvelled at Susan's lack of fear. While she trembled to face a patroness at Almacks and quailed before Lord Ailsa's crusty demeanour, she hadn't the slightest compunction about penetrating the mysteries of a deep, damp cave!

"That's why we brought the lantern, Susan," said Lord Hastings, swinging it for all to see. "Perhaps I'd best light it now."

"I suppose you know what lies ahead?" asked Felicity.

"In fact we do. There's higher ground just in a little way where the sand is dry. We can sit and tell ferlie stories, eh, Miss Bell?"

At Lord Hastings's teasing grin, Felicity merely shrugged and tried to look bored.

"I wish to hear about the saint and the beastie," chirped Susan. "I suspect it's quite a story!"

"Rather a myth," Felicity emphasized dampeningly. "As you must know, Susan, all stories about loch beasties and sea monsters are mythical in nature." She looked again at Lord Hastings, fully expecting an argument. He chose not to comment, but rather appeared thoroughly involved in lighting the lantern wick.

"Are they only myths, Kyle?" Susan turned wide, trusting eyes to her fiancé. Felicity sighed. Susan would believe anything Kyle told her.

"Och, it's for everyone to decide for himself, Susie, lass. Mayhap once I tell ye a story or two, ye can make up yer own mind!"

Lord Hastings had lit the lantern, and began to lead the way into the darkness. Instead of offering his assistance, he had simply grasped Felicity's arm and tucked it against his side. Under other circumstances, Felicity would have objected to such a proprietary gesture, but decided that now was not the time. As they progressed further inside the cave and away from the opening's light, Felicity was grudgingly thankful for the earl's comforting closeness. She pulled her shawl snugly round her, grateful now that she had been obliged to bring it.

Presently Felicity's shoes no longer squished along the damp cave floor. They were walking on sand.

"This is as far as we go," said the earl, lifting his lantern to shine on the granite wall in front of them. "Spread the blanket, Kyle, and I'll pop the cork! Here, Miss Bell, hold the lantern, won't you?"

Felicity automatically accepted the lantern. "Pop the cork? Pray tell, Lord Hastings, what are you talking about?"

Kyle unrolled the blanket, exposing a wine bottle, and a large work candle and holder, which had been hidden inside. He handed the bottle to Lord Hastings, who immediately set about dislodging the cork, while Kyle shook out the blanket and spread it over the sand.

Susan clapped her hands in delight. "Champagne! Oh, Kyle, how clever of you! But we haven't any glasses!"

"Look here, lass. Never say the Kennedys dinna come prepared!" Kyle reached into his coat pockets and plucked out two small goblets.

"But that's only two glasses, Kyle," Felicity pointed out.

Kyle looked at Lord Hastings. "Jamie, dinna ye bring some glasses?"

"What? And take up all the room in my pockets? Where would I have put these?" Lord Hastings reached into a pocket with his free hand and pulled out an apple and two plums. Felicity saw how easily his large hand cupped all three pieces of fruit, and an unexpected quiver ran down her spine. Goodness, his hands were large! But they weren't oafish-looking at all. The fingers were slim and long. She remembered how they'd spanned her waist yesterday after the infamous carriage accident.

"Don't look so stricken, Miss Bell," advised the earl. "I've more fruit in the other pocket."

For a dreadful moment Felicity had the ridiculous notion that Lord Hastings knew what she'd really been thinking. Observing him now from beneath her cautiously lowered lashes, she still wasn't sure. His black eyes taunted her.

"I wasn't lamenting the lack of fruit, my lord," she informed him. "As your cousin said this morning, I've not the need for vast quantities of food to sustain me. But I do wish you'd brought more glasses!"

"Susan and Kyle can share," said Lord Hastings, dismissing the problem with a wave of his hand. "And so can we," he added.

Felicity looked mildly irritated and gracefully lowered herself to sit on the blanket. "Then I shall do without!"

Susan let loose a trill of laughter. "Goodness, Felicity, you were not always such a goose! What a fuss you're making! I begin to suspect that you are becoming more like Henry every day!"

This criticism stung Felicity more than anything else Susan could have said, though she had to admit that Susan was right. She was being absurd. Had it been anyone other than Lord Hastings...

"I'll drink on one side of the goblet and you can drink on the other, Miss Bell," said Lord Hastings. "Never fear, our lips will never touch—" he paused and Felicity's eyes flew to his face "—the same spot on the goblet's rim," he finished, his brilliant black eyes wide and ingenuous in the lantern light.

"Very well!" she said, loathing the snippishness in her voice but unable to control it.

The others sat and Felicity was dismayed to discover the earl right next to her and much too close. He sat Turkish style, his long legs crossed in front of him. One knee rubbed against Felicity's thigh whenever either of them happened to move. She tried to rearrange herself so as not to be thusly irritated by his lordship's encroaching knee, but to no avail. Since the two men were veritable giants, the blanket was barely large enough to hold them all.

Kyle poured the champagne, the effervescent bubbles a fitting accompaniment to Susan's delighted gurgles of laughter. Felicity grimly observed her sister, reminding herself that it was for Susan's sake she was making this sacrifice of spending so much time in Lord Hastings's company.

Kyle handed Lord Hastings a glass of champagne, which his lordship immediately offered to Felicity. "Ladies first," he said, bowing his head with exaggerated gallantry.

"Thank you," said Felicity. She took the glass and sipped a tiny amount and promptly returned it to the earl. Much to her chagrin, he made a great show of turning the glass round to sip from the other side. After a couple of swallows, Lord Hastings turned the glass round again with painstaking exactness.

"There you are, Miss Bell!" he said, handing her the goblet. "The chastity of your lovely lips will not be sullied by any fault of mine!"

Felicity could not help herself. She laughed. "How ridiculous you are!"

Lord Hastings raised his brows.

"And so am I!" admitted Felicity. This time she more thoroughly quenched her thirst. To be sure, it had been rather a hot walk to the cave. But now the cool cave and the champagne eased away any discomfort caused by the heat. If only she could dismiss the *other* source of her vexation.

"Kyle, tell us about the beastie and Saint... What was his name?" Susan looked as happy as Felicity had ever seen her.

"Saint Columba," supplied Kyle. "Aye, lass, 'tis the oldest written testimony of the Loch Ness beastie." He handed a nearly full glass of champagne to Susan while he readied himself to tell his tale. Leaning forward, he began in a lowered voice.

"'Twas early in the fifth century when Saint Columba came to northern Scotland to spread Christianity among the heathens. In his travels one day, he found it necessary to cross the River Ness. When he came to the bank thereof, he saw some locals burying a poor, unfortunate man. They told Saint Columba that only moments before a water monster had snatched at the man while he was swimming in the river!''

"Goodness, how dreadful!" breathed Susan, then she took a bracing swallow of champagne. Felicity frowned. Susan never dealt well with wine, and so much of it this early in the day did not seem wise. But how was she to alert her sister without Lord Hastings accusing her of meddling?

"Aye, and he was bitten with a most savage bite!" Kyle continued, his Scottish love of tale-spinning quite evident. "His hapless corpse was dragged aboard a boat by men who'd come to lend assistance. But they were too late!"

"How sad!" said Susan, shaking her head.

"Indeed," agreed Kyle. "But it might have been worse. Seeing that Saint Columba was in need of a boat to cross the river, a devoted follower of the Blessed Man—Lugne Mocumin by name—cast himself into the river to fetch one from the other side. Now the beastie, which was not so much satiated as made eager for prey, was lying hid on the bottom of the river. But perceiving that the water above was disturbed by the faithful but foolish Lugne, the beastie suddenly emerged. Swimming to the man, it rushed up with a great roar and open mouth!"

Probably too enthralled and delightfully frightened to speak, Susan sucked in a large breath of air, then hiccupped.

"The Blessed Man looked on, while all who were there, the heathen as well as the brethren, were stricken with very great terror. With his holy hand raised on high—" Kyle demonstrated "—he formed the sign of the cross in the empty air, invoked the name of God, and commanded the fierce monster, saying, 'Think not to go further nor touch thou that man. Quick, go back!' On hearing the voice of the saint, the beastie was terrified and fled backwards more rapidly than it came, as if dragged by cords. It had come so near to Lugne as he swam that there was not more than the length of a punt pole between them!"

"No doubt there were a great many converts to Christianity that day," Felicity commented dryly.

"Aye, Felicity," agreed Kyle, not the least daunted by her sceptical tone. "Seeing that the beastie had gone away and that their comrade, Lugne, was returned to them safe and sound, the holy brethren glorified God. The barbarous heathen, who were also present, were constrained by the greatness of the miracle they'd seen with their own eyes, and likewise glorified the God of the Christians!"

"Who records this account?" Felicity asked. "Saint Columba himself?"

"Nay, lass," said Kyle. "Saint Adamnan wrote the Blessed Man's biography, devoting an entire chapter to Saint Columba's expulsion of the water monster."

"And what other miracles are credited to Saint Columba?"

"I see what you are about, Miss Bell," Lord Hastings interjected with a knowing smile. "And to be perfectly fair, it must be said that Saint Adamnan's biography of Saint Columba was written more than a century after Columba's death, and is a frankly adoring account replete with many miracles and fabulous tales. In his time, Saint Columba is supposed to have busied himself by raising folk from the dead, sailing against the wind, curing all manner of ills and magically opening locked gates."

"There!" said Felicity. "Now I am satisfied." She turned to Susan. "Obviously another myth, Susan."

"But I wish to hear more," Susan insisted, her face flushed with excitement and, no doubt, the champagne. "Do tell more, Kyle!"

Kyle sat back, leaning on his hands. "'Tis your turn, Jamie!"

"Och, Kyle, there's no following such a tale," Lord Hastings said, his words laced with that delightful Scottish burr again. Felicity stared at him, wide-eyed. Did he even realise that he experienced these lapses?

"Tell the lasses about the beastie Morag!" Kyle urged.

"Aye, Morag," murmured Lord Hastings. "Well, there's not much to tell, really. Only that 'tis said the beast exists. And one might well understand the per-

sistence of such a belief amongst the people who live
near the eerily enchanting banks of Loch Morag. The
craggy mountains which shadow the loch's deep,
crystal-clear waters are most often shrouded by mist.
Huge island hummocks dot the loch. 'Tis a fitting
dwelling for a loch beastie.''

"Do ye remember the song, Jamie?" prompted
Kyle.

Lord Hastings black eyes narrowed in concentra-
tion. "Aye, I think I do."

Then, to Felicity's utter astonishment, Lord
Hastings began to sing. His voice was a softly penetrating baritone, quite appropriate for the forebod-
ing song.

"Morag, Harbinger of Death,
Giant swimmer in deep-green Morar,
The loch that has no bottom...
There it is that Morag the monster lives.

"I'm afraid 'tis all I remember," he apologized at
the end of his extraordinary performance.

"It is quite enough! I'm sufficiently daunted!"
Susan assured him. "Now I dare *not* believe in loch
beasties, or I shall be frightened out of my wits!"

Felicity was shaken by his lordship's song, as well.
But not by the words, or any sort of connexion with
the beastie, Morag. Lord Hastings's deep, spell-
binding voice had stirred her senses. It was as if she
were a harp and he the master of her melody. She was

a taut string at the command of his caress. He had only to strum his lean fingers along the length of her and she would sing. . . .

"What say ye, Miss Bell?" enquired Lord Hastings, when she continued to stare speechless. "Are ye still a non-believer?"

"In beasties?" she enquired, distracted.

"Aye, lass! What else?" he said.

Felicity shook herself. "Yes!" she stated flatly. "It is a complete humbug, in my estimation. A monumental fudge! No sensible person could believe such a Banbury tale!"

Kyle sighed and smiled with good humour. "Give over, Jamie. The lass is too English!"

Felicity chose not to take offence at this explanation for her disinclination to believe Scottish folklore, and this was no time to reflect on her reaction to Lord Hastings's song. Susan was drinking another glass of champagne and it was her duty to stop her.

"Susan, how many glasses have you drunk?" she enquired disapprovingly. "Don't you think you've had enough?"

"This is only my third! I'm not an infant, you know!" Susan returned passionately. "You're always treating me as if I were, Felicity, and I do wish you'd stop!"

Felicity was stunned and silenced. She supposed the wine must account for Susan's rudeness.

Susan stood up, swayed slightly and giggled. "I feel delightful, Kyle! Come, let us walk on the beach. I want to feel the spray of sea-water on my legs!"

"Whoa, lass," laughed Kyle, rising to steady her in his arms. "Have a care, now. We'd best proceed slowly."

"Shall we come and bring the lantern?" Lord Hastings offered. "Or will you light the candle?"

"Do you wish to come?" Kyle asked.

"Well, I'm about to eat an apple. I should not like to come just now," Lord Hastings admitted.

"The candle it is," said Kyle. "Light it for me, Jamie."

"I really think I ought to come along, Kyle," said Felicity, beginning to stand up. "Susan seems a bit—"

"Do you suppose Kyle is not capable of taking care of Susan?" Lord Hastings enquired mildly, while he removed the lantern chamber and lit the candle.

Felicity flushed. "'Tis only that she's a trifle foxed, you know and—"

"Do you plan to escort them on their honeymoon, Miss Bell?" persisted the earl, his tone still mild but pointed. Having finished his task, he fixed his keen gaze on her. "Perhaps Susan will drink a tad too much of the wedding toasts and will need your assistance then, as well!"

Felicity sat back down and seethed. Lord Hastings handed the candle to Kyle, who then supported and guided his giggling fiancée out into the sobering sunlight.

"I'm sorry to be so blunt," said Lord Hastings. "But you do not seem to take a hint very well!"

Felicity would not look at him, but she could hear him crunch into his apple. "Perhaps I'm not completely convinced you have an accurate assessment of the situation!" she returned bitingly. But tears stung against her eyelids and doubt twisted painfully in her chest. Susan *had* accused her of treating her like an infant. She'd also compared her to *Henry!*

"Well, perhaps I do not," allowed Lord Hastings. "But then again, perhaps I do."

"Oh, you!" Felicity fumed. "You make me so angry!"

"So you've said before," Lord Hastings replied. "And since you're already angry with me, I might as well say something else which will anger you."

"Carry on, sir," said Felicity through clenched teeth. "I don't suppose you could be any ruder if you tried!"

"You underestimate my powers," replied the earl teasingly. But then he sobered. "Let me ask you a question, Miss Bell. Why haven't you married? I should think a beauty such as yourself ought to have been asked a time or two."

"I've been asked several times!" she retorted.

"Then I repeat, why haven't you married?"

"Why? What has *that* to do with Susan?"

"Well, I have begun to think the only real and lasting cure for your propensity to meddle in your sister's life, and perhaps in the lives of others you have affection for, is to have a family of your very own. With no children to direct and scold, love and admonish, your talents are being quite wasted."

"Perhaps, Lord Hastings, I haven't married because I don't want a man continually telling me what to do! Your gender seems to think ruling the roost their god-given right! You're a perfect example, you know!"

"Might I suggest that your fears reflect just the opposite, Miss Bell? Perhaps you shun marriage because you're afraid you'll end up telling your *husband* what to do. And that would sink him in your opinion forever."

Felicity had had quite enough. She was holding back a most unladylike urge to box his lordship's aristocratic ears. And the worst of it had been his uncanny explanation for her inability to find a suitable suitor. She naturally was drawn to malleable fellows, so she could do as she pleased. But as soon as they bowed to her superior strength of will, she despised them. Obviously, marriage to someone you despised was out of the question.

Not that marriage was necessary for happiness. In fact, she'd been inclined to believe just the opposite. But always in the back of her mind she'd wondered if perhaps there existed a perfect mate for her. Perhaps if there were... She shook herself. Such fairy-tale nonsense did not bear thinking of!

Felicity rose and presented Lord Hastings with a most composed, queenlike visage. "I wish to leave now."

While he still sat on the blanket, finishing the remains of his apple, it wasn't that difficult to imagine him kneeling in the manner of a loyal subject in her queenly court. The idea pleased her so well that she went further still. She imagined him kissing her bejewelled hand, pledging his allegiance to die for Queen and country—or at least to indulge her every whim! Perhaps if she pictured him thusly, she could imagine despising him, too.

Alas, it was not to be. Lord Hastings would not co-operate. He laughed. "Bravo, Miss Bell! Bravo!" he cried, pulling himself up to his full, imposing height. "Queen Elizabeth lives again! But it will never do. Try as you might, you'll never rule me. While I'm a reasonable man and open to suggestion, I shan't be led about by the ear!"

Felicity weakened under the influence of such an exultant look. No, she'd never rule him. Drat the man. Now he was more attractive than ever!

CHAPTER EIGHT

THAT EVENING HUGO still had not made an appearance at the castle, nor was any message received explaining his delay. This seemed further proof that he had not been given the note left for him at Gretna Green. Picturing the pandemonium which must have ensued upon Hugo's return to Heathwood without his mistress, Felicity shuddered. But her family's distress would not be of long duration, since the letter she'd posted to them would come fast on Hugo's heels.

No doubt they would be shocked to learn of her hey-go-mad decision to travel with the earl, but she'd had no choice. And as nothing had happened...

Felicity frowned into the mirror as Meg styled her hair. Nothing had happened, she repeated to herself. But was that strictly true? Certainly the earl had not tried to seduce her. Despite his teasing, he'd been a perfect gentleman. Physically, he'd not touched her, but he'd made a sludge-puddle of her brain!

She had always known him to be arrogant, but this morning at the sea cave, he had quite exceeded her expectations by the way he'd demanded to know why she hadn't married! And then to suggest that marriage was a cure for her meddling! Meddling, indeed! But when he went so far as to suggest that instead of fearing that she'd be ruled by her husband, she was afraid *she'd* rule *him, that* had been the outside of enough! No one had ever dared say any of these things to Felicity before, and she was thrown into a quagmire of confusion.

"The seamstress left a satin ribband to match yer gown, miss," said Meg. "Shall I weave it through yer hair?"

"Yes, please," answered Felicity. The gown the seamstress had sewn so expeditiously was lovely. The white muslin was sprigged with peach-coloured flowers and trimmed with ruching of the same shade. The sleeves were puffed, with a deep flounce of peach lace falling to below her elbows. Since she'd been so restricted in her clothing of late, Felicity felt quite luxurious having another change of dress.

Meg stepped back. "Do ye like it, miss?"

As usual, Meg had worked her magic. Except for a few wisps of delicate curls framing her face, Felicity's hair was swept back into a glossy knot, with long, shining ringlets falling from the back to rest on her slender shoulders. The ribband was weaved fetchingly throughout.

"Once I leave here, I don't know how I shall go on without you, Meg!" exclaimed Felicity, smiling. "But you are a godsend for Susan!" Meg was very pleased and Felicity sent a happy girl away to her dinner in the servants' dining hall.

Felicity sighed. Now she supposed she ought to descend to the drawingroom and to her own dinner, but she dreaded the evening. After their adventure to the sea cave, Susan had been obliged to sleep off her wine, and Felicity had declined a game of piquet with the gentlemen and had also adjourned to her bed-chamber.

While it had not been necessary to sleep off an over-indulgence in morning champagne, Felicity had been too angry with Lord Hastings to partner him in cards. But after pacing her room for an hour, she'd calmed. She'd even gone so far as to consider his lordship's words.

Now she was forced to admit that perhaps there was something in the things which he had said. Perhaps she ought to let Susan fend for herself. And mayhap she *was* reluctant to marry for fear of both being ruled *or* ruling absolutely! She sighed again. There ought to be a happy compromise between the two!

But hiding thus in her bedchamber was to no purpose. It was already seven o'clock, Geddes's usual time for bellowing "dinner!" from the drawing-room threshold. Remembering one of her mother's frequent admonitions, she must be a "brave soldier and face the dragon." Felicity smiled ruefully. Or was "beastie" a more apt description of her dragon? Either way, she'd best go down. The men were undoubtedly sharp set, their bottomless Kennedy stomachs clamouring for more food!

Felicity picked up her reticule and fan and left the room. She hesitated at the top of the stairs when a sudden thought came to her. What if he was right about *everything?* It was a possibility she had to consider. But in that case, must she then cease to be angry with him? Oh, Lord! Then she'd have no defence at all! Felicity descended the stairs feeling more frightened and beyond control than she'd felt in the entire course of her five-and-twenty years.

FOR ONCE LORD HASTINGS'S hunger was overshadowed by a more pressing concern. Felicity was late to dinner. Had he so discomposed her that she was unwilling to face him? But that was impossible, wasn't it? The lass was more pluck to the backbone than most women put together. And she was intelligent and would consider his words rationally—he was sure of it.

But the earl could not but feel uneasy. He hoped he had not been too blunt with her. He did not wish to hurt her. He wished merely to give her a helpful hint or two. He did not suppose he was all knowing or anything so ridiculous, but sometimes when a person was too close to a problem, as Felicity was close to Susan, he or she couldn't see things clearly. In such a case, an objective person was much more able to offer advice. He only wanted to be of help.

Lord Hastings leaned against the mantelpiece, broodingly contemplating the dancing firelight reflected in his brandy glass. But was he really *objec-*

tive? He swirled the amber liquid round and round and wondered how he'd managed to forget his bachelor's creed and somehow attached himself to a woman. It certainly was not his intention to buckle himself to a wife at the tender age of three-and-thirty. He had not done sowing his wild oats!

Beyond light, meaningless flirtations, he'd always managed to steer clear of entanglements with that most fearsome of creatures, the "respectable female." But none of them had had quite that shade of red hair, he acknowledged, smiling to himself. Or eyes the colour of a new spring leaf. Or skin as pure and delicately textured as a baby's bottom! But her skin smelled a dammed sight better than *that!* Like roses—dew-bathed roses. By gad, he'd even got poetic!

But there was more to her than her astonishing beauty. She was bright, quick-witted, full of humour and love and, God knows, she was definitely capable. Her streak of stubbornness and that compulsion of hers to manage the lives of everyone about her were her only faults.

But they were considerable faults, the earl reminded himself sternly. And certainly nothing he would care to deal with for thirty or more years of marriage! And it was entirely possible that upon further, more intimate, acquaintance with the lady, he'd find even more faults hidden beneath that beautiful facade!

"I'd give much to be privy to yer thoughts, lad," interrupted Lord Ailsa. Lord Hastings looked up to discover his grandfather standing nearby, toasting his back at the fire. He hadn't even noticed his grandfather's closeness until he was spoken to.

"Nay, Grandfather, ye dinna want to know," he said ruefully.

Lord Ailsa's eyebrows lifted. "Aye, now I want to know more than ever! Ye've slipped into the Scottish brogue! Most often ye do it when ye're feeling some sort of strong emotion, or else when ye're spinnin' a tall tale!"

"Devil a bit, do I still do that? What a confounded nuisance!" grumbled Lord Hastings, taking care to sound as English as the Lord Mayor of London himself.

"Makes perfect sense, lad. Until yer mother hired that English governess, ye were allowed to speak just as ye pleased. And ye pleased to speak like yer mother! A darlin' lass, Janet! Naturally, even now ye slip back into the brogue when ye're speaking from here." Lord Ailsa placed his hand over his heart.

"Well, I do not wish to be dictated to by that particular organ of my body, Grandfather," Lord Hastings said firmly. "I will listen only to my brain!"

"What's yer brain sayin' now, Jamie?" Lord Ailsa's gaze had strayed to the drawingroom door. His voice lowered to a whisper. "Or can ye hear it above the beating of yer heart?"

Lord Hastings turned towards the door and was struck speechless. That is, until he muttered the decidedly Scottish exclamation "Blether!" Then he shook himself, and willed his traitorous heart to calm. Good gad, if only she weren't so beautiful! And tonight she looked even a little vulnerable, which served only to ignite his protective instincts. She seemed unusually self-conscious and a bright flush of colour blossomed on that petal-soft skin.

Lord Ailsa walked eagerly forward to escort the blushing beauty into dinner, while Lord Hastings looked on, feeling the veriest country bumpkin. Kyle and Susan were summoned from a remote window seat by Geddes's earsplitting dinner announcement, and Lord Hastings followed reluctantly behind. He did not wish to sit beside Miss Felicity Bell at the table. She smelled too good. Good God, he did not know if he could even eat properly!

Lord Hastings stopped in his tracks, the deep frown on his face observed with surreptitious interest by the two footmen flanking the door. Things had definitely gone too far if he could not even eat! He had better remove himself from Miss Bell's intoxicating presence before he turned to mere skin and bones!

"I STILL THINK ye ought to fetch the toothdrawer!" said Kyle, laughing. "Naught else but the toothache could so dampen Jamie's appetite!"

They had removed to the drawingroom en masse, since neither Kyle nor Lord Ailsa wished to linger over their port. Felicity hadn't the slightest idea what Lord Hastings's opinion had been about abandoning this deeply ingrained male ritual. It seemed he had no opinion at all. She'd never seen him so taciturn. In fact, he hadn't contributed to the conversation one jot during the entire meal, except to reply briefly to questions directed specifically to him.

This left Felicity and Lord Ailsa to engage in a veritable tête-à-tête, since Susan still could not bring herself to discourse with Kyle's grandfather without trembling and spoke only to Kyle, who, in turn, spoke only to her.

But most remarkable, Lord Hastings had shown a marked decline in appetite! Of course, he wouldn't starve. He'd still eaten more than she had, but it was a considerable reduction to his normal amount. What was the matter?

"Jamie does'na need a toothdrawer," Lord Ailsa stated. "He pines for a little Scottish dancing, eh, lad?"

"I wish the lot of you would cease speculating about my supposed lack of appetite," complained the earl wearily. "Even horses are allowed to be off their feed for a day or two without inspiring this much concern! I'm a little preoccupied, if you must know. I've just recalled a pressing engagement and must be off the minute your vows have been exchanged, Kyle!"

"What pressing engagement is this?" asked Kyle, genuinely surprised. Yes, thought Felicity, what pressing engagement? When they were at The Bull and Crown he'd mentioned an appointment, but she'd heard nothing more about it since. Had Lord Hastings simply wearied of her company and wished to be off with all due haste?

She watched Lord Hastings and wondered at the sudden distant expression on his face, as if he'd withdrawn himself from them already. Or at least from her. He caught her looking at him and she turned quickly to say something to Susan.

While her back was turned to Lord Hastings, Felicity heard him whisper teasingly, "Never you mind, Kyle. 'Tis not such a topic as ought to be discussed in front of ladies!"

Felicity felt the heat rise in her cheeks. Mayhap he'd not meant for her to hear his words to Kyle, but she had. And she could only assume that he was speaking of a liaison with a doxy, or some such vulgar woman gentleman feel compelled to visit from time to time. Perhaps he had a mistress in keeping and was loath to neglect her. She felt a pang of jealousy. No, it wasn't exactly a pang. Rather it was more like a huge, green beastie breathing tissue-searing fire deep within her! Goodness, how had she come to such a pass?

"Remember, lads, day after tomorrow ye'll be expected to participate in the Sword Dance and the Fling," said Lord Ailsa, not to be distracted from his purpose. "I doubt not ye're both a little out of practice. Ye'd better try the steps again once or twice. We'd best go outside, though, or else the two of ye might shake the floor to pieces! There's daylight enough left."

"But we can't practice without pipes, Grandfather," objected Kyle. He looked longingly towards the windows at the soft twilight bathing the out-of-doors in an aura of romance. No doubt he would rather take Susan for a walk than join Lord Hastings in a dance.

"Ye dinna wish to shame yerself in front of the whole clan, do ye, Kyle?" enquired Lord Ailsa gruffly. "I'll play the pipes!"

Kyle looked resigned. Felicity darted a quick glance at Lord Hastings. He did not appear so much resigned as annoyed. But apparently neither of them wished to disappoint their grandfather.

In truth, Felicity was rather enthralled at the prospect of watching Kyle and Lord Hastings participate in such an activity. She wondered if Lord Hastings would don a kilt. Lord Ailsa answered that question for her immediately.

"Choose a kilt from my wardrobe, Jamie. Be quick about it! And I'll fetch my pipes!" Lord Ailsa's eyes shone with excitement as he strode from the room.

A footman was dispatched to fetch a blanket for the ladies so that they could sit on the grass and watch the proceedings in comfort, while the men saw to their own preparations. Felicity and Susan walked outside and had just settled their skirts about them on the blanket when the men appeared at the castle door.

At the sight of Lord Hastings in a kilt, Felicity was considerably shaken. While Kyle looked well enough in the masculine skirt, Lord Hastings seemed born to wear it. He had discarded his jacket and neckcloth and had his shirt-tail tucked into a green tartan kilt. His shapely calves were encased to the knee in tartan stockings and he wore flat, buckled slippers.

Felicity watched him cross the lawn to where they sat, the kilt swinging from his slim hips most provocatively, then suddenly realized her mouth was open! But apparently Lord Hastings hadn't observed her distressing lack of control. In fact he hadn't even glanced her way. Where was the teasing banter? she wondered, feeling a twinge of disappointment. It was as though he was bent on ignoring her!

Felicity forced herself to look away from Lord Hastings's virile figure and determinedly fixed her gaze on the others. Lord Ailsa was toting bagpipes and Kyle carried two swords, which he laid on the grass. Evidently they would do the Fling first.

The men conversed with each other for a few minutes, then Kyle and Lord Hastings positioned themselves side by side and with perhaps two arms' lengths between them, to commence dancing. Lord

Ailsa blew a few discordant practice notes, then began the melody.

Despite the widely held, rather cynical view that bagpipes are best if heard from a distance, perhaps accompanying a military formation cresting a hill, Felicity was spellbound by the haunting strains flowing from Lord Ailsa's bagpipes. And as for the dance, the agile movements of the two men were fascinating. She'd never seen the Fling performed before, and was greatly impressed with its precision and meticulous form.

Lord Hastings and Kyle stood upright throughout, their backs never bending, while they vigorously executed arm and leg movements and kept lightly on their toes. Felicity watched closely and concluded that the dance had got its name from the "fling" which served as a break between steps on first one leg and then the other.

Whatever were their feelings upon first being compelled to practice the dances, now Lord Hastings's and Kyle's faces reflected nothing but pure enjoyment. Occasionally they misstepped and laughed heartily about it, slapping each other on the back and renewing their efforts with ever better results.

Several servants had been lured from the stables, and even from the house, to gather about and watch the two cousins perform. Ale was fetched to quench the dancers' thirst and revivify the piper, whose face had grown decidedly red in the past half-hour.

Presently they prepared to do the Sword Dance. Lord Ailsa confessed himself winded, and one of the servants, a hearty-looking fellow, received the bagpipes and set about his task of playing them with alacrity. The Sword Dance was of nature more sober and the movements slower and more fluid.

Felicity found herself mesmerized by the dance and by the whole mood of the evening. She was filled with a sense of kinship with the Scots (servants and nobility), as she sat thusly in the strange, seductive charm of twilight. The long shadows of the dancers reached far across the lawn, their swords glinting softly in the muted glow of the sun, which was half-immersed in a crimson sea.

Then there was an abrupt change of mood when Lord Ailsa suggested they end the practice on a lively note by performing the Shantruse. The Shantruse was a dance created in celebration of the return of the kilt after the long decades during which it had been prohibited. Lord Ailsa explained to Felicity that the dancers would mimic kicking off imaginary trousers, the hated symbol of oppression.

Lord Hastings and Kyle were joined by several of the servants in dancing this particular jig, accompanied by a great deal of laughter and friendly shouting.

Finally everyone had reached a pleasant state of exhaustion, and fell to the ground to rest. Lord Ailsa mingled with the servants, asking about their spouses and children. Kyle collected Susan and returned with her, arm in arm, to the castle. Felicity was content to stay exactly where she was, enjoying every last nuance of twilight. But shortly this did not prove entertainment enough, and she found herself closely watching Lord Hastings as he walked about the lawn.

Without conscious volition, Felicity's eyes scanned the length of him. From his muscled calves in their tight tartan stockings to the narrow hips and broad chest, he was as finely hewn as a Greek statue. The damp ends of his black Kennedy hair curled against his collar. His nose was classically straight, and his firm lips stretched over white teeth as he smiled and conversed with what undoubtedly were not only servants, but fellow clansmen.

Suddenly he was returning her gaze. Even from the distance of several feet, Felicity was frightened, as well as stirred, by the intensity of his look. First he had ignored her all evening, then when she took a fancy to scrutinize him, just as he had done her on numerous occasions, he finally noticed her! She knew with a certainty that the minute he could politely end the conversation he was having, he would come to her.

Standing abruptly, Felicity walked away quickly across the lawn towards the nearby woods. Now that she had got his attention, she had no desire to tangle with Lord Hastings! She was feeling too muddled to be an able adversary in a match of wits. She had little choice but to flee!

Skimming the edge of the loch (or the beastie's spawning pond, whichever it was!), Felicity paused for breath, leaning against a tree.

"There you are!"

It was all Felicity could do not to shriek. But she ought to have known he would follow her into the woods. He had come up close behind her and now he leaned over her, one hand propped against the tree, exactly level with her head.

"Good heavens, Lord Hastings, must you sneak up on a person? You frightened me half out of my wits!" She spoke lightly, hoping he did not suspect how she trembled. She couldn't move. He stood too close.

"You expected me to follow you, Miss Bell." It was a statement of fact, not a question.

"I don't know what you mean!"

"Look at me, Felicity!" It was a command, not a request.

Felicity looked at him. First his chin, with its stubborn thrust and deep cleft, then his firm lips, dewed with a hint of perspiration. She shivered. Finally her gaze settled on his eyes, those fathomless pools of velvet darkness.

"Has anyone ever told you, Miss Bell, that such a thorough scrutiny of a man, such as that you gave me on the lawn a while ago, and such as the one you just now enjoyed, is a clear invitation?" Lord Hastings's voice was low and teasing, but with that undercurrent of passion she suspected he barely held in check. His intense gaze captivated and compelled her.

"An . . . invitation?" she repeated stupidly.

A low, amused, slightly cynical laugh rumbled from his chest. She watched his shirt-front rise and fall, and felt his warm, pleasantly ale-laced breath on her face. "Yes, my dear Miss Bell. Tonight you send out a most unmistakable invitation. You want me to kiss you!"

Felicity sucked in her breath. Her pulse beat wildly, deafening her to every sound outside of their intimate circle. "I . . . I did not mean t-to encourage you, my lord, I . . ."

"No, you did not mean to encourage me," the earl agreed, his mouth curved in a sensuous half smile. "Your wiles are of the most dangerous variety. They are perfectly innocent, and you barely understand them yourself. But they are deuced potent, Miss Bell! Have a care, my dear. Confirmed bachelor rakes like me take advantage of innocents like you."

At first Felicity had been sure that the earl meant to kiss her, which was thrilling and frightening. Now she suspected he had only meant to teach her a lesson, which was condescending and maddening! The odious man! She was not a child and she would prove it!

"'Tis not enough that you needs must advise me about my sister and the suitability of marriage to curb my meddling, Lord Hastings, but now you lecture me on flirting and the dangers thereof!" she said disdainfully. "I am a twenty-five-year-old spinster, practically an ape-leader! You don't frighten me in the least!"

To Felicity's great satisfaction, Lord Hastings was taken aback. And while she had him thus off guard, she thought to prove herself undaunted by his condescending and quite unnecessary lecturing. She wasn't afraid of him *or* his kisses! She threw her arms about his neck, pulled his face down to hers and kissed him full on the mouth.

However, Felicity hadn't expected such a explosion of sensation to rush through her body at the mere touch of his lips to hers! If she could judge by the bemused expression on Lord Hastings's face, he'd felt something, too. And like Saint Columba's ancient water monster, this beastie was not satisfied with a taste; his appetite had been merely whetted!

Black eyes flashing, Lord Hastings pulled Felicity firmly into his arms and crushed her against his chest. He possessed himself of her lips and nearly bruised them with the passion of his kiss. Such passion was frightening enough, but it was her own ardent response that alarmed Felicity most.

When he finally released her, it was a gradual process. His lips trailed lingering caresses across her face while his arms lessened their hold by degrees. Suddenly, she felt him withdraw completely. When she opened her eyes, he had gone. She blinked once or twice until her eyes focused properly. Had she dreamed it all? No, there he was, standing by the loch. His back was to her, his face averted.

"Lord Hastings?" Why was he standing thusly? Did he despise her? Was she a wanton in his eyes?

"Go back to the castle, Miss Bell!" His words were clipped.

"But...why?" She felt confused, hurt.

"Just go!" It was a uncompromising command. Now Felicity felt more than hurt. She felt angry! She hurried back to the castle, resolved never to speak to Lord Hastings again as long as she lived!

FELICITY HARDLY SLEPT that night. She tossed and turned, ever seeking that magic spot on her pillow that would send her into dreamless sleep and banish Lord Hastings's image from her mind. But to no avail. Whether her eyes were closed or open, whether she reclined or paced, his black Gypsy eyes haunted her. And even worse, the sensations of ardent delirium which had coursed through her body when he held her and kissed her, returned full force at the slightest recollection of the event.

Now she stood at the window and watched the sun slowly inch its way into the sky, scattering mist in its wake. The swans on the pond stretched and fluttered their wings in morning ablutions. The weather promised to be fair, but despite the cheerful aspect from her window, Felicity did not greet the day with enthusiasm. The wee, dark hours of the night had revealed something to her. Something terribly disturbing. She was in love!

The realization was shocking. Having progressed so far into spinsterhood, Felicity had never expected to fall in love. In fact, she had begun to think herself immune. After all, despite her many suitors, none of them had inspired even the slightest twinge of desire to abandon her pleasant single existence for marriage.

She tried to rationalize her feelings, blaming the earl's considerable expertise in matters of passion against her relative inexperience. Of a certainty she would be overwhelmed by such a thorough kissing. But such a simple explanation would not do. As an experiment one Season, she'd braved the risk of scandal and had allowed three separate men of her acquaintance to kiss her. She was forced to admit the results of the experiment sadly disappointing. But at least she then knew that if kissing was so dreadfully insipid, she need not regret missing the more intimate activities allowed by marriage. Now she was not so certain!

However, it was not merely the earl's physical appeal which had flung her headlong into love. He had some very special qualities besides. He was kind, chivalrous, discerning, intelligent and full of humour.

Felicity frowned. Yet he was arrogant, a persistent tease and as meddlesome as herself, in many ways! If they married, they would butt heads continually. He would not be a complacent lap-pug, that was a certainty.

Since he was basically a fair-minded man, he'd probably allow her most freedoms she'd desire in the wedded state. But she was equally convinced that from time to time he'd put up a daunting opposition to some scheme or other, and she'd have to fight tooth and nail to get her way. And in the end, perhaps she'd not get her way at all!

Felicity smiled. For some reason, such a prospect did not seem at all unpleasant. She could do with a challenge now and then.

But such speculating was to no purpose. Lord Hastings had made it quite clear that he was not the marrying kind. He was a seasoned rake and even now was anxious for Kyle and Susan's wedding to be over so that he could return to his mistress! His curt dismissal of her last night was certain proof of his aversion to matrimony. He probably thought himself bound to offer for her now that he had truly "sullied the chastity of her lips," as he had said jokingly at the sea cave yesterday.

Tears pricked against Felicity's eyelids. Nevertheless, she took a deep breath and made a resolution. Much as she now would welcome a proposal of marriage from Lord Hastings, she must refuse him if he were to ask. An unwilling bridegroom would never do. Felicity whisked away the tears until there were too many to manage, then she let them fall unheeded. No, an unwilling bridegroom would never do at all.

CHAPTER NINE

DRESSED IN SUSAN'S emerald green riding habit, altered to fit her, Felicity was just rising from the dressing table when there was a soft knock at the door. Susan hurriedly entered the room, saying abruptly, "Felicity, why did you not come down to breakfast? I need to talk to you! Something dreadful has happened!"

Susan looked and sounded extremely agitated, but Felicity was determined not to show alarm. And not just because there was a servant in the room, but also because she'd resolved to stay out of Susan's affairs. Besides, she was too weary from lack of sleep and low spirits to be much alarmed by anything. Probably Lord Ailsa had discomposed her sister at the breakfast table and Susan had broken something valuable.

"Thank you, Meg," said Felicity, dismissing the girl with a smile. Meg returned her smile shyly, curtsied to them both and left the room.

"I had a light breakfast much earlier in my room," Felicity replied to Susan's first question. "Now, come sit down beside me on the chaise where we can have a comfortable coze," she continued, taking care to be as calm and casual as possible. "I am so glad the seamstress sent the riding habit over promptly, as she said she would. The day is so fair that one is loath to sit indoors a second longer than necessary!" Felicity sat down on the chaise and patted the cushion beside her invitingly.

Susan eyed her sister in some considerable confusion. "Felicity, didn't you hear me? I've something dreadful to tell you. Do stop rattling on that way. I have need of you!"

Felicity sighed, resigned at least to listen to Susan's complaints. But she would not meddle. She was *determined* not to meddle. "Carry on, Susan," she said with affectionate weariness.

"As you know, we planned to ride this morning. And I was so looking forward to it!" began Susan, pacing the floor.

"Are we not riding?"

Susan heaved an exasperated sigh. "But of course we're still riding, but *he's* coming along!"

"Do you mean Lord Hastings? I had assumed he would."

"No, not Lord Hastings! Well, yes, Lord Hastings is coming, but it is Lord Ailsa I refer to! He means to join us today! Felicity, will you tell them I've the headache? If I must ride a horse in Lord Ailsa's company I shall surely mortify myself!"

Gazing into her sister's pleading, distraught eyes, Felicity couldn't help but pity her. The lack of progress Susan had made so far in trying to overcome her fear of Lord Ailsa seemed to portend disaster today. Normally Susan was a neat little horsewoman. She'd even joined the hunt a time or two in Yorkshire and performed creditably. But with her nerves in a tangle, there was no telling how she'd fare.

Felicity was tempted for a moment to accommodate her sister. It might be dangerous for Susan to mount a horse in such a state of agitation. Had she ought to meddle just once more? But no, she would not! Kyle was well able to take care of Susan.

"Susan, don't be absurd, dearest. Kyle will help you with the horse, if you should need help," she responded soothingly. "After all, you have ridden since you were out of leading strings. There's naught to worry about!"

Felicity stood up and lifted a hat from the bed. She stood in front of the mirror and placed it carefully on her head, trying to appear unconcerned.

"Felicity, is that all you have to say?" demanded Susan, probably completely crushed by her sister's apparent desertion. "You know what a clodpole I can be!"

"I also know how charmingly graceful you can be," returned Felicity, fixing her sister's gaze in the mirror. "Yesterday you said you wished me to cease treating you like an infant, Susan, and I am determined to oblige you.''

"You're angry with me, then?'' Susan accused tearfully. "I had had too much champagne when I said that to you, Felicity. I didn't know what I was about. I meant to apologize! Surely you don't hold that against me?''

Felicity turned round and gently grasped her sister's shoulders. "Indeed not, Susan,'' she said kindly and earnestly. "You were quite right. I *have* been treating you like an infant. And my misguided attempts to help and protect you have probably contributed as much to your lack of self-confidence as anything!''

Susan squirmed loose and moved to stand with her back to Felicity. "I still can send Meg to tell them I'm ill, you know. I don't really need your help at all,'' she said in a muffled voice.

"Yes, you certainly may send Meg to tell them you are ill,'' Felicity agreed matter-of-factly. "It is entirely up to you. From now on I leave you to make your own decisions, Susan. I have enough faith in your upbringing and your own good sense to know that you will invariably make right decisions.''

Felicity smiled wryly to herself and added, "Well, perhaps you will make an occasional mistake. We are all of us apt to be very stupid from time to time!''

Susan sniffled loudly and Felicity opened a drawer of the dressing table and withdrew a single handkerchief from a fluffy mound of several and slipped it over Susan's shoulder.

Susan took it and blew her nose vigorously. Felicity gave her sister's shoulder an affectionate squeeze. Presently Susan calmed and bade Felicity goodbye in a rather sulky voice.

Felicity had no idea whether Susan would ride with them. She'd been a little tempted herself to plead indisposition in order to avoid Lord Hastings. But she found herself wishing to see the earl as much as she wished to avoid him! Being in love was rather confusing, she decided.

LORD HASTINGS'S HORSE pranced and sidled, its hooves ringing on the courtyard cobbles. "Whoa, boy! You're a fresh one, ain't you?" he soothed, caressing the smooth neck of the magnificent roan with one hand and holding the reins of a chestnut with the other.

"A real bo-kicker, that roan," agreed Kyle. He, too, was mounted and held the reins of a grey intended for Susan. "Almost as bad as this one! But I like a spirited bit of blood!"

As if to give credence to Kyle's words, his black stallion reared up. Kyle laughed and settled the horse with a firm pull of the reins.

Lord Ailsa rode up just then, saying disapprovingly, "Kyle, I dinna know ye meant to saddle

Demon. He's hardly broke yet. Mayhap ye ought to saddle another.''

"I can handle Demon, Grandfather," Kyle assured him a little haughtily. They still were not on the best of terms. "Besides, here come the ladies now!"

Lord Hastings braced himself and turned to watch Felicity and Susan approach them, or to be more precise, watch *Felicity* approach them. She looked damned fetching in that emerald green riding habit! The colour suited her perfectly, as did the close, military cut of the trim jacket and skirt, nipped in at her small waist and flared at the hips. The matching hat was trimmed with a flirtatious black ostrich plume which curled up and over the rim to caress her blooming cheek.

Despite his firm resolve to control his passions this day, Lord Hastings could not seem to hold the sudden desire he had to fling himself down from the horse and repeat last night's embrace. He had had to send her back to the house to avoid further intimacies between them. Her response to his kiss suggested she was as attracted to him as he was to her, and it was not wise for the two of them to be alone together. Because he respected her enormously, he would keep his passions firmly in check till the wedding night!

Last night had been a revelation. The feelings she stirred in him as he held her in his arms were much more than physical. After all, he'd been attracted to her from the moment he'd first seen her at The Bull and Crown. But holding her as he had done last night had made him realize that she belonged to him entirely, and for always. The mere idea of another man ever holding her and kissing her in such a way nearly drove him mad.

He had need of her in his life. Like the rose with its inevitable thorns, Felicity was both beautiful and prickly. To smell the heady scent, one had to risk a few thorns for the pleasure. Life would never be dull or predictable with such a feisty lass! He loved her.

But while such a strong emotion held him in its grip, he endeavoured to keep any trace of it from appearing on his face. He knew she desired him, but he still did not know whether she loved him. He would discover the state of her heart at the first private opportunity. When their eyes met, though hers glittered strangely, the couple only exchanged brief, polite nods.

He dismounted to assist Felicity, and found it easy enough to toss her lightly into the saddle, but certainly much more difficult to let go of her once she was seated. His hands slid away from her waist reluctantly. He watched as she curved her knee over the pommel and arranged her skirts, then remounted his own horse, cursing under his breath. The rigid set of her lovely mouth revealed that she was angry with him—that was certain. How he longed to explain himself! But he had to wait.

Lord Hastings was anxious to be off, but it seemed that Kyle was having difficulty helping Susan to mount. He would toss her up and she would awkwardly grasp at the pommel to right herself, then slide down again into Kyle's waiting arms.

This unfortunate display was repeated four times before Susan succeeded in balancing herself in the saddle. Her face was red with embarrassment by now. And Kyle's face was red, too, but it was obvious to Lord Hastings that his cousin's heightened colour was due to an earnest effort to stifle his merriment at the situation. Kyle was too kind to laugh, knowing that it would probably make Susan feel worse.

Lord Hastings noticed that Felicity made a point of looking away. She had not tried to interfere at all. He eyed her speculatively.

At last they were off. Their plans were to ride along the north road through the moor and over to a meadow in the woods where Lord Ailsa had had fences erected for jumping.

Kyle and Lord Ailsa rode on either side of Susan, and Felicity kept behind with Lord Hastings. He wondered at her restraint. Normally she would have included herself in the conversation of the others, jumping in whenever she deemed it necessary to explain Susan's meaning in order to avoid Susan's sinking herself lower in Lord Ailsa's regard.

Lord Hastings observed her composed profile with interest. Was she taking his advice? His heart swelled with affection, and he felt more eager than ever to confess his love to her.

He deliberately slowed his horse's pace and watched to see if Felicity would follow suit. When she saw what he was doing, she looked very much annoyed and a little nervous, too. But she fell in step. Presently, once the others were sufficiently distanced, he spoke.

"Miss Bell, about last night... I wish to apologize—" he began.

"Don't apologize," she coolly interrupted him. "I've already forgotten about last night. As far as I'm concerned last night did not occur."

Lord Hastings raised his brows. She'd already forgotten about last night? He certainly hadn't, and he would wager every shilling in his possession that she hadn't, either!

"Miss Bell," he began again, injecting a bit of good-humoured cajolery into his voice. "You make it deuced difficult for a gentleman to apologize to a lady for his reprehensible conduct!"

"But I don't want your apology!" she informed him quite firmly, turning towards him just long enough for him to observe her flashing eyes. "I kissed you first, remember."

This was not going precisely as he'd planned. Lord Hastings persevered. "But I kissed you second. And you must admit, it was a much more thorough kiss than the first! I owe you an apology, Miss Bell.'' His voice lowered and softened. ''And furthermore I wish to tell you that—''

''I've been kissed by any number of men before you, Lord Hastings!'' she blurted out, her face flushed with delicate colour. ''You needn't feel bound to uphold my honour. I did not require it of *them*, after all.''

Lord Hastings drew himself up stiffly. He was appalled! How dared any man touch Felicity! He was filled with rage and jealousy! He knew he was being quite unreasonable, but he couldn't seem to help himself.

Their eyes locked for an endless moment. Fear and challenge were mixed equally in Felicity's expression.

''I don't believe you,'' Lord Hastings said at last. ''But even if you are speaking the truth, it doesn't make the slightest difference to me.'' He sincerely meant that, too. He would wipe her memory clean of anyone who had ever kissed her before! He took a deep breath and began. ''Miss Bell, will you do me the honour of—''

''Please don't offer for me, Lord Hastings!'' She reined in her horse and turned towards him. Lord Hastings halted his horse, as well, and now they faced each other. Felicity's smile seemed forced and her eyes were a little too bright. ''It is quite unnecessary, you know. We've crossed miles of country together. We've even slept in the same room! Just because you've kissed me is no reason to...to doom us both to a loveless marriage! Besides, I have no wish to marry, now or ever!''

Lord Hastings felt as though he'd been slapped across the face. A bee swooped and buzzed between them. The sun beat down through the dappled shadows of an overhanging tree. The day was still as fair, but for Lord Hastings everything had changed. She didn't love him.

''Very well, Miss Bell,'' he said at last, wrenching his eyes away from hers. He could not help the bitter edge that crept into his voice. ''I shall not further discommode you with my repugnant offers of marriage.''

A small sound something like a moan escaped Felicity, but Lord Hastings urged his horse forward. Felicity followed just behind. Breaking into a canter, they soon caught up with the others.

FELICITY TOOK THE FIRST fence easily. Approaching the next, she tightened her right leg against the crutch, leaned forward and sailed over with inches to spare. She urged her horse to go faster. Pushing her strength to the limit and testing her skill seemed to help Felicity fend off the rising tide of despair which threatened to engulf her. She had too much pride to allow herself to break down in front of the others.

Having completed the run, she trotted back to where the others, still mounted, were gathered beneath the shade of a large oak tree. She carefully avoided Lord Hastings's eyes.

"Blether, Miss Bell!" exclaimed Lord Ailsa admiringly. "Ye're a rare bruiser on a horse!"

Felicity forced a bright smile, and said breathlessly, "Princess is a fine filly. She has good bottom!" She stroked the horse's neck.

"Are ye sure ye dinna want to try it?" Kyle asked Susan. "Just the first fence or two? Felicity says ye're a bonny rider, lass."

Susan darted a glance at Lord Ailsa and shook her head. "No, Kyle, I don't think so. At least not today."

Kyle looked disappointed and Lord Ailsa resigned. Felicity sighed deeply, but she would not interfere.

"Are ye ready for another run, Jamie?" asked Kyle, holding his skittish horse with a firm hand on the rein.

"You go first. Your horse is champing at the bit. I'll follow you," said Lord Hastings without much enthusiasm.

Felicity glanced at him from beneath her lowered lashes. He'd seemed awfully subdued since she'd rebuffed his offer of marriage. He ought to have been elated. And he ought to have been grateful! A woman of less principle would have taken advantage of his sense of honour and accepted his offer, disregarding his aversion to marriage.

Kyle rode out several yards and turned to face the first fence. There was no need to urge the horse to a gallop. He had merely to give Demon free rein and they were off. The way the beautiful black stallion sailed over the fences was a sight to behold. Lord Hastings watched for a minute or two, then rode out in the opposite direction to build up speed for jumping.

Felicity watched him go, her heart thrilling and aching at the same time. He looked so well in his buckskin breeches and brilliant black boots, turned down at the knee to reveal white tops. His tailcoat was burgundy, the colour she favoured on him. His waistcoat was a reserved floral brocade, and as usual, his cravat was tied to perfection. As for the way he sat a horse, she was quite sure Wellington could not have done better.

"No! Kyle!"

Felicity was startled out of her bittersweet reverie by the sound of Susan's terrified scream. She jerked her head towards where Kyle had been riding, and all she could see was Demon, prancing and whinnying, his elegant head tossing this way and that. Kyle had been thrown!

Felicity just barely recognized what had happened when a royal blue habit on a grey horse streaked past. Susan was going to Kyle, riding neck-

or-nothing towards the first fence. Since Susan had very little time to prepare for the jump, Felicity feared for her sister's safety. She was about to cry out, warn Susan against attempting the jump, but she stopped herself. It was better not to distract her at this point. Besides, Susan was a good rider and she ought not to interfere.

She held her breath as Susan jumped the fence, and then the next and the next. Finally she reined in where Kyle had fallen and neatly dismounted before the horse had even come to a full stop.

By the time Felicity and Lord Ailsa had got to the scene of the accident, Lord Hastings had already arrived. Kyle's head was cradled in Susan's lap and Lord Hastings knelt over them. He was giving his cousin the same sort of examination he'd given Felicity when they were thrown from the gig. Though Kyle looked a little dazed, they were all relieved to see he was conscious!

"Does it hurt anywhere particular, lad?" asked Lord Ailsa, kneeling on the other side of Kyle.

"Nay. It hurts everywhere!" he admitted, chuckling weakly.

"Naught's broken," said Lord Hastings at last. "Too bad this happened the day before your wedding, cousin. You'll be too sore to, er, dance the Fling tomorrow!"

He'll be too sore to do anything tomorrow, thought Felicity. And that was precisely what Lord Hastings was implying! She blushed.

"You underestimate the Kennedy will, cousin," Kyle returned with a devilish gleam in his eye. "Where there's a will, there's a way!"

Felicity looked at Susan to see if she was understanding any of the innuendo the wicked Kennedy lads were bandying about, but her sister's eyes were fixed in concern on Kyle's face.

"You ought to have listened to your grandfather, Kyle," Susan admonished him, smoothing his hair. "You allowed that he didn't wish you to ride Demon. And now you know why!"

Kyle looked sheepishly at her.

"Aye, lass. He's not one to listen to his grandfather," said Lord Ailsa, a new respect glimmering in his black eyes as he watched Susan. "But perhaps he should not in all things for I sometimes make mistakes!"

Susan looked at Lord Ailsa a little uncertainly, but she didn't tremble. Finally she was able to return his warm gaze, and even to smile.

"I hope you'll forgive an old fool and give me another chance to welcome ye to Culzean, and to the family," Lord Ailsa continued. "I know I haven't made the way easy for ye thus far!"

"Lord Ailsa, I understand. You were concerned for Kyle. It comes of loving him so much! And I plead equally guilty to such a weakness. There's naught to forgive.'' Susan reached forth her hand and Lord Ailsa promptly clasped it affectionately between his two.

Felicity closed her eyes and sighed in relief. Finally Lord Ailsa and Susan had come to an understanding. They had a very special common regard: their love for Kyle. And regardless of how many things she'd broken or cups of tea she'd spilt, Lord Ailsa now knew that Susan could be spirited and strong enough to stand as his grandson's wife. Felicity had a feeling that henceforward Susan would find it much easier to be graceful in Lord Ailsa's company.

When Felicity opened her eyes, Lord Hastings was looking at her. Forgetting all that had passed between them just an hour before, Felicity smiled. In his responding smile she saw that he was just as pleased and relieved as she was, as if Susan were his own sister. But, after all, they *would* be cousins. How Felicity wished they could be more! She felt her eyes well with moisture and turned hurriedly away.

Lord Hastings cleared his throat and said kindly, ''Susan, I had no idea you were so pluck to the backbone!''

''Well, and so I told you both,'' said Kyle, grunting and struggling to his feet with the help of both the other men. ''Drat, how I wish the ground would stay still!''

"I don't think you ought to ride, Kyle," said Lord Hastings, concern wrinkling his brow. "Sit yourself down again and I'll fetch a carriage to cart you home, old man!"

Kyle obeyed, but Felicity could tell he was loath to be so helpless, especially the day before his wedding!

Lord Hastings rode off, pulling the still skittish Demon alongside by his tethers. Felicity's eyes followed him till he was a speck on the road. She never tired of watching him. And she might as well do so while she could. After tomorrow he would be gone back to his estate in Devon by way of the abode of a certain ladybird. Felicity sighed heavily.

FELICITY WAS SO EXHAUSTED from her sleepless night and the high drama of the morning that she took a three-hour nap before dinner. When she awoke, her heart was heavy. She'd been dreaming about *him*. But she refused to co-operate with her own misery and rang for Meg, determined to maintain her composure despite everything.

She had a revivifying bath and gave Meg full office to dress her hair as she pleased. Meg had borrowed a copy of *The Lady's Magazine,* and copied a style called *à la Sappho.* To Felicity, the style seemed almost too daring for someone with her particular shade of hair. It consisted of nothing more than a mass of thick ringlets falling from a single twist of hair at the crown.

Aunt Mathilda would say she looked like a doxy. But, thank goodness, Aunt Mathilda was in Yorkshire. And her aunt ought to have got her letter by now. If all went well, Hugo would be back with her carriage by the day after tomorrow.

"Since there's company, ye'll be wantin' t'wear yer new sprigged muslin, won't ye, miss?"

Felicity stared. "What company is this, Meg?"

"Och, dinna ye know, miss? Ye must have been asleep through all the excitement! It's yer aunt, a Miss King, I think they said."

"Good God, Aunt Mathilda!"

"And your brother."

"Henry, too?" Felicity felt as if every breath of air had been squeezed out of her. "How long have they been here, Meg?"

"Not more'n an hour, miss," Meg answered, her eyes wide as she observed Felicity's obvious agitation. "They've been shown to their rooms and all. 'Spect ye'll see one another at dinner."

"But who met them?" She hoped Lord Hastings had been spared their hysterics.

"I dinna rightly know," confessed Meg. "Wish't I could tell ye more, miss. But all I heard in the kitchen was that the visitors—beggin' yer pardon, miss—had raised quite a humdurgeon!"

Felicity covered her face with her hands. "Oh, no," she moaned.

"Miss, are ye all right?" asked Meg. "I would'na ha' told ye about it if I knew it was goin' to upset ye!"

Felicity sat up straight. "No, Meg. You were quite right to tell me. Now I shall be better prepared. Yes, I'll wear my new gown. Make haste! I had better go down straight away. Possibly I can spare my gracious host some harassment from my well-meaning *meddlesome* relatives!"

Felicity dressed quickly and hurried down to the drawingroom. When she first entered the room her eyes were drawn to Lord Hastings, who leaned negligently against the mantelpiece. His tall, straight form, clad in elegant black evening clothes, was always first to command her attention despite whoever else might be present. She pulled her gaze away from him to observe the other occupants of the room.

Lord Ailsa was likewise standing by the fireplace and Kyle was half-reclined on a chaise, his long legs crossed at the ankles. He seemed paler than usual and a little drawn about the mouth.

Henry faced Lord Ailsa, a glass of brandy in one hand. If only he did not look as if he'd recently been sucking on a lemon, he might be deemed a handsome man, thought Felicity. He was nearly as tall as the Kennedys, though considerably thicker through the middle. His ginger hair was peppered with grey.

And as for Aunt Mathilda, perched erectly on the edge of a chair, she looked to have recovered from her cold and seemed desperately eager to be helpful in whatever capacity was granted her.

Susan was absent, giving Felicity reason to believe that she and Susan had been excluded intentionally, in all probability in order that the others could better discuss them.

"Felicity! Dearest child!" exclaimed Mathilda upon spying her niece. Then she sprang from the chair like a frog from a lilypad and scurried across the floor to embrace Felicity. "You cannot imagine what we've been through, my dear. When Hugo turned up at Heathwood without you, I was beside myself!"

Felicity returned her aunt's embrace, then gently moved her aside and faced the others. "How do you do, Henry?" she greeted her brother. She was not usually so formal, but she was angry. Then before he could reply, she said, "Why are you all here, excepting myself and Susan? You aren't discussing us as if we were naughty little pea-hens who ran away from school, are you?"

"Don't kick up a dust, Felicity," her brother advised in his sonorous, stern voice. "We were—"

"I thought you were in London seeing to Emma's tooth," Felicity interrupted.

Aunt Mathilda left off frowning at Felicity's coiffure to say, "Henry came home early, Felicity. Little Emma's tooth was spared. Forgive me if I boast a little, but it was my special mix of herbs which did the thing. All she had to do was wash out her mouth three times a day, swishing back and forth, you know, and—"

"I went to Heathwood as soon as I had got my family settled at home," Henry said, curtailing what undoubtedly would be a rather long monologue from Aunt Mathilda. "Hugo had just returned from Gretna and your aunt was apoplectic. It took me a while to piece together the story while listening to Hugo and Aunt Mathilda, both of whom persisted in speaking at the same time and neither of whom were the least calm! But once I deduced that both of my sisters had turned into Bedlamites, I was off to Scotland in a trice!"

"Then I assume you left England before my explanatory letters arrived," said Felicity. "A shame that you went to all this fuss and bother for nothing! But how did you know how to get here?"

"We travelled to Gretna thinking to discover what we could from innkeepers and the like," Henry said. "Once we ascertained that you had stopped at The Anvil, a Mr. Gordon gave us precise directions to Culzean."

"Mr. Gordon has rather a deplorable habit of being helpful only at the most inconvenient moment, wouldn't you say, Miss Bell?'' Lord Hastings offered dryly.

''Indeed,'' Felicity murmured, allowing herself only a brief glance at Lord Hastings. ''He certainly failed me when he did not deliver my note to Hugo!''

She wondered if her brother and aunt had been pressuring the earl to marry her? It seemed very likely so, and she was mortified and stiff with tension.

''Come, lass, sit down,'' ordered Lord Ailsa in a kindly voice. He walked over and placed a hand under Felicity's elbow and guided her to a chair next to Kyle. ''Ye're right, lass. We had'na ought to discuss and make decisions in yer absence.'' He turned to Geddes and bellowed, ''Fetch Miss Susan, will ye, Geddes?''

Aunt Mathilda and Henry flinched, not as yet used to the shouting.

Felicity's eyebrows lifted. ''Surely there's nothing more to discuss and certainly no decisions are left to be made,'' she said cautiously. She turned to Henry, who persisted in wearing his Friday-face. ''Henry,'' she began in a reasoning voice. ''The gentlemen must have told you everything. And since Susan and Kyle are to be wed on the morrow, I see no reason for you to be acting the prig!''

Henry turned as red as a chokeberry. ''Good God, Felicity, have you forgot all your notions of decency? Certainly Susan's affairs have been settled.

Lord Ailsa and I deem the match a good one on both sides, and marriage settlements are to be drawn up on the morrow. Concerning these things, I am satisfied. But what of you, missy? What shall be done about you? You spent two nights of your journey quite alone with this gentleman." Henry flung an arm in Lord Hastings's general direction.

"As well you know, Henry, nothing untoward happened!" exclaimed Felicity. "And since the only people who know of my travels with the earl are in this room, I do not see the harm."

"Oh, Felicity! Don't be angry, my dear," twittered Aunt Mathilda, twisting her handkerchief fretfully. "But you must know, the vicar and Miss Priscilla Prudey were at Heathwood when Hugo called me from the room to tell me you'd likely been abducted. I could not help it, dearest, I screamed! Then, I fainted dead away. When I came to, I must have babbled senselessly." Aunt Mathilda braved a peek at her niece. "They know all, dearest!"

Felicity dropped her head into her hands, muttering, "Not Vicar Sowerby and that gabster Miss Prudey! I shall be the main topic of conversation in every parlour in Thirsk by the end of the week!"

"Likely much sooner than that," Henry observed grimly. "And the on dit will certainly be carried to London, as well. Now do you understand my concern, missy?"

Felicity did not reply. Silence hung heavily about her like wet socks on laundry day. Gradually she lifted her head from her hands and peered round the long ringlets which fell forward against her cheeks. Everyone was observing her. She lifted her chin, her innate sense of pride restoring her courage. "I don't care what people say! I know I did naught wrong. Let them believe what they will!"

"Felicity, you're being mulish!" scolded Henry. "Even Lord Hastings agrees that you and he ought to wed. He has his own sense of honour to consider, you know!"

Felicity tossed the ringlets which obscured her view and observed Lord Hastings. He hadn't moved an inch from where he stood when she'd first entered the room. And he'd barely spoken. If only she knew what he was truly thinking!

She studied him, the languid ease with which he propped himself against the mantelpiece. He appeared relaxed enough, except for his eyes. They glittered with a strange light. And while his slight smile was mocking, it looked strained and forced. Felicity decided he must be trying to hide his disgust. It was too much!

"Where are you going, Felicity?" Aunt Mathilda cried, as Felicity stood up and hurried from the room. She nearly ran into Susan in the hall and drew a startled gasp from Geddes, who only saw a white streak and a blur of titian curls whiz by. She let her-

self out by the front door and ran to the ornamental
pond. There by the cool water she hoped to find
sanctuary from the painful feelings which plagued
her.

CHAPTER TEN

LIKE PRISMED GLASS, golden twilight shimmered all around Felicity. Her shadow on the pool's surface stretched like a distorted mirror in front of her, an elongated body with a tiny head. Seagulls glided on the warm, still air, and crickets sang their rhythmic chants to the pale, low-floating moon.

Felicity stood and stared into the reflective waters. She was ashamed of herself for running off like a silly heroine from one of those rubbishing novels from the lending library! All sensibilities and no sense!

Well, perhaps she wasn't quite as silly as they were. The Evelinas and Dominiques who lived between the pages of novels frequently exposed themselves to unfriendly elements, such as downpours and lightning storms, or flung themselves head-first into rivers or down from precipices. All in the name of hopeless love!

Felicity smiled despite the ache in her heart. She was much too sensible to do any of those silly things. She would simply sit for a few minutes and be utterly miserable. Then she would return to the castle and apologize for her behaviour. But while he did not love her, she would not, could not, marry Lord Hastings.

Felicity eased herself down on the grass and tucked her feet beneath her. A few small rocks fringed the edges of the pond. Since the swans were not enjoying the water at the moment, Felicity picked up one of the rocks and tried to skip it across the pond's placid surface. Unfortunately, she found she had not the skill. Each time she tried, the rock fell heavily into the water with a decided *plunk*.

"'Tis in the wrist, Miss Bell. Just so."

Felicity turned her head quickly and discovered Lord Hastings several feet away. He pressed and polished a rock between his thumb and forefinger, then threw it across the gleaming green water. It skipped three times before it *plunked*.

"And it helps if you choose a rock that is relatively flat." Lord Hastings began to walk slowly towards her, and Felicity's heart beat frantically. Why had he come? To convince her to marry him? Very likely—but for all the wrong reasons!

"Lord Hastings, I hope you are not intimidated by my starched-up brother," she began nervously. "I told you at The Bull and Crown that you should not be obliged to marry me if it was discovered that we travelled together. And I am as good as my word! Henry cannot make me marry you!"

Lord Hastings now stood directly over Felicity. Her eyes strayed from looking at the pond and saw one of his polished slippers not three inches away from her knee. There also was a strong ankle and a muscular calf in an impeccable stocking. She would look no farther. She refused to be beguiled by his lordship's obvious physical attractions. She returned her gaze determinedly to the water.

He stooped, balancing lightly on his toes. Now his face was quite close, so close that she could feel his breath on her face. "Look at me, Miss Bell," he commanded.

Slowly Felicity turned her head. Meeting his eyes straight on was most unnerving. The brilliant black depths drew her in. The inky pupils were like dancing sylphs to Felicity's fascinated imagination. They seduced her.

"Why won't you marry me, Miss Bell?" he asked, his voice a cajoling, silken baritone. "I'm probably no worse than most men. Can't you do so even to preserve your reputation?"

Felicity was about to tell the truth. She was about to tell him that she wouldn't marry a man who didn't love her—not to save her reputation, not for any reason. The fact that *she* loved *him* made it all the worse. But she caught herself and mumbled, "Blast my reputation! There are many reasons why I don't choose to marry you, my lord."

"For example?" he prompted.

"For example, because I do not choose to place myself or my fortune under the restraint of an . . . an arrogant man!" She flashed him a challenging look. "And because . . . because I am too old to change my ways to suit you. And because you don't—" Felicity bit her lip. No, she would not say it!

Lord Hastings cocked his head slightly and considered her thoughtfully. "I don't what, Miss Bell?"

"It is of no consequence," she sighed, rising and walking away to rest her head against the trunk of a tree. He followed her and stood just behind.

"This may seem quite a surprise to you," Lord Hastings began slowly. It seemed as though he was choosing his words with great care. "But I really don't wish you to change your ways to suit me." He cleared his throat. Then, in a voice barely audible, "Actually, your ways suit me well enough already."

Felicity's heart fluttered. She raised her head slightly. What was he saying?

"And as for your fortune . . . Risking the chance of sounding a braggart, I'm quite flush in the pockets as it is! You will have just as much ready as ever, you know." He cleared his throat again, giving the distinct impression he was nervous.

"As for my arrogance, well . . ." he gave a short laugh. "That can't be helped any more than you can help being stubborn!"

Lord Hastings's entire manner seemed most unusual to Felicity. He had almost the air of a hopeful
suitor! She wished it were so! She hoped it were so!

"Why are you so willing to marry me, pray tell?"
she asked him carefully. "I should think you'd be
delighted at my stubbornness in refusing to marry
you. You told me yourself you are a confirmed
bachelor!" She tensed, waiting for his answer, all her
hope of happiness resting on his response.

Felicity felt, rather than heard, Lord Hastings approach still closer. "Have you considered how uncomfortable your position will be when you return to
Yorkshire, Miss Bell?" he asked earnestly. "People
can be cruel, you know. Even in London they will
gossip. Your honour is at stake, and you entrusted
me with your honour when we set out from The Bull
and Crown together." He paused and when he resumed speaking his voice held a distinct tremor of
regret. "It would make me miserable to be the cause
of such trouble!"

Felicity's budding hope withered. If pity for her
and a sense of honour were his only reasons to marry
her, she must still refuse him. A moment earlier she
had begun to think he felt something more. "'Twill
be nothing but a nine days' wonder, my lord," Felicity assured him dully. "Miseries of such short duration are trifling compared to a lifetime of misery
brought about by a mismatch between you and me!"

Felicity heard the earl curse under his breath. Suddenly his large hands roughly clasped her shoulders. "Do ye really think we are so incompatible, Miss Bell?" he said gruffly. He pushed aside a ringlet and brushed his lips lightly against her nape. Felicity shuddered exquisitely.

"I assure ye, lass, I would try mightily to be a good husband to ye!" He kissed her neck, trailing his lips across a bared shoulder. "Of course that does'na mean I would let ye order me about like a lap-pug, but I would not order ye about, either!"

Felicity remembered vaguely that at one time she'd thought of the comparison with the lap-pug, too. Moreover, she'd also noticed that Lord Hastings had slipped into the Scottish brogue! He seemed to do that when his feelings ran high, or when he was telling a tall tale! Which was it this time?

Lord Hastings turned her round, and slowly, almost reverently, pressed his lips against her forehead. Then he kissed the tip of her nose, each hollowed cheek and finally her chin. By the time he had done with this exquisite accounting of each feature, Felicity felt like a mass of quivering flesh. His lips hovered just above her own.

"And if it's love you want, lass," he whispered huskily, "someday I swear you'll love me as desperately as I love ye!" Then he lowered his mouth and captured her lips in a fierce kiss. Felicity clung to him helplessly, her mind reeling.

Several euphoric moments later, she pushed him away. "What did you say a moment ago about l-loving me?"

"Felicity, sweetheart," he groaned, enfolding her in his arms and crushing her against his broad, warm chest. "I know you dinna love me, but I think you might learn to love me by and by. There's never been a woman who's affected me as ye do! Why, I haven't been able to even eat properly since yesterday when I first kissed ye! I'll be skin and bones! Have pity, sweetheart. Marry me!"

Lord Hastings suddenly was aware of a rather convulsive movement against his shoulder, as if Felicity were crying. "There, there, lass," he crooned. "Dinna fret!"

Felicity raised her laughing face from his shoulder. "You beastie! I should have known you'd find some way to bring food into the conversation! But you needn't plead with me to save you from starvation. I love you, too!"

Words were insufficient to express Lord Hastings's heartfelt happiness. Lifting Felicity off the ground, he swung her round and round in dizzying circles, his exultant whoop of joy echoing across the lawn.

At the castle, Aunt Mathilda rushed to a window facing the formal grounds. Peering into the growing darkness, she exclaimed, "Good heavens! He must be killing her! I've never heard such a noise! Come here, Lord Ailsa! Listen!''

Lord Ailsa walked over and leaned into the window embrasure. He listened, then he smiled hugely. ''Nay, Miss King. He's not killing her, he's wooing her!'' Then he gave her a broad wink and sauntered away.

Aunt Mathilda shivered. This sort of savage courtship must be Scottish in origin. Goodness, she thought, not only was Lord Hastings too tall, his Scottish half seemed too much in evidence as well!

EARLY THE NEXT DAY, there was a double wedding at Castle Culzean. Though Susan wore white and Felicity wore bright yellow, each dress boasted a sash of Kennedy tartan.

Lord Hastings danced the Fling while Kyle looked on enviously. But while Kyle might have been well enough to join in the dancing, he'd soberly informed Lord Hastings that he was conserving his energy for when it could be needed later on.

With his large hand firmly holding her up at the elbow and ensuring against accidents, Lord Ailsa introduced Susan round to all the clansmen. Susan was charmingly polite to each and every face that swam before her in an endless stream.

By the end of the day, she felt very much a part of the vast and friendly Kennedy Clan, and more than a little grateful to Lord Ailsa for his steadfastness. A bond was forged between them which promised to endure. Felicity saw how well things progressed, and was thankful.

Despite Aunt Mathilda's prejudice against tall men (especially tall men in kilts), she seemed to enjoy the festivities as much as anyone. When she danced the reel with Lord Ailsa, a high-pitched trill of laughter escaped her spinster's throat, leaving no doubt as to her enjoyment of the activity.

With the help of a little wedding punch, even Henry unbent. By the end of the day he was forced to admit that both sisters had got themselves admirably buckled despite the ramshackle way they had gone about doing so. He was even resigned to losing the kindred spirit, Wenthorp, as a brother-in-law.

To Felicity's delight and alarm, Lord Hastings was determined to leave the party before the day was much progressed. He seemed extremely anxious to spirit Felicity away and have her all to himself. They would make a short stop in Yorkshire to collect her belongings and dash off a wedding announcement to the papers, and then continue on to Lord Hastings's estate in Devon.

On the journey south, Felicity was pleased to discover her husband's appetite returned to its former vigour. Apple cores and orange rinds flew from the carriage windows with daunting regularity.

When he wasn't eating, Lord Hastings extracted from Felicity every detail of her life until the day they met. And, in turn, he obliged Felicity by narrating his own existence from boyhood to manhood. If he left out certain details, such as the numerous women he must have wooed and won over the years, Felicity didn't mind at all.

He did, however, explain why it was more important than ever that he keep his "appointment." He had done with mistresses forever! By the time they pulled up to The Ferry and Ferlie, they were much better acquainted with each other—but no less in love.

If Mr. Stuart found it odd that the young woman introduced to him as Lord Hastings's sister a few days before was now most proudly declared to be Lord Hastings's bride, he did not reveal it by so much as the blink of an eye. In his long career as an innkeeper, he must have heard and seen much odder things. However, his instincts told him that the former Miss Calamity Denham was now most assuredly a countess. But just to be sure, he asked them if they'd be needing the cot.

"No, Mr. Stuart, we will not be needing the cot!" Lord Hastings assured him in so emphatic a tone that Felicity shivered. She was reminded of earlier speculations about his lovemaking, never dreaming at the time that one day soon she would know for a surety whether he was passionate. Pondering on the many contradictory tales she'd heard about the marriage bed, Felicity admitted to herself she was a little frightened.

But over dinner, when Sally served the meal with as much eye-batting and hip-swinging as she had done formerly, Felicity had a distinct pleasure in knowing that she was sharing his lordship's bed, and not Sally. It was also most gratifying to observe that Lord Hastings barely registered the serving wench's presence in the room. He was much too absorbed in Felicity.

So Felicity prepared for bed philosophically determined to endure, for the sake of marital harmony, whatever unpleasantness was required of her beyond the admittedly enjoyable activities of kissing and embracing.

The next morning, Felicity sat on the window ledge, alternating her view of placid Loch Doon with the view of her sleeping husband, sprawled across the bed. She was still in her nightdress, a diaphanous peach confection assuredly not designed for warmth.

While it was a very pretty view of the loch and it was a delightful, fair day, Felicity found herself much more enthralled with observing her husband. He lay on his stomach, one arm thrown across the bed where Felicity had been lying. The bed covers were in telling disarray, one side pulled across him just far enough to preserve modesty. His smooth, muscled back was exposed and so was one long, bare, black-furred leg.

Waving ebony hair, much too long to suit the Beau, fell across the white pillow in a tumble. Felicity remembered how her fingers felt twining through those luxurious strands. She remembered other things, as well, and her stomach flip-flopped. She knew now just how wonderfully passionate her husband was, yet how gentle, too, when it was important to be gentle.

Felicity puzzled, her smooth brow furrowing slightly. How could anyone possibly describe lovemaking as a wifely "duty"?

Suddenly she noticed a movement below on the lawn. Looking down, she observed several people running towards the loch. Her curiosity piqued, she threw open the window and called out to one of the maids she recognized from the inn. "What is happening? Where is everyone going?"

"Och, miss! Ye ought t' come down! There's stirrin's in the water near the sands. One of the stablelads said he saw the beastie disportin' itself in the loch! Come and see!" Then the excited maid ran off.

Astonished, Felicity stared after her. She was tempted to dress and join the throng, if for no other reason than to assure herself that nothing but an odd-shaped log had surfaced to give the local believers a thrill. She closed the window, stood up and moved towards the wardrobe.

"What's the commotion, my love?" came a deceptively drowsy voice from the bed.

Felicity turned to discover her husband's black eyes fixed upon her. This was the first time he'd seen her in bright daylight with so little on. He missed nothing in his keen perusal. As his eyes raked over her, Felicity shuddered with rekindled desire.

"Something was seen in the water, Jamie. A beastie disporting itself in the loch, they say," she mumbled. He shifted on the bed, turning to reveal the fine, crisp curls of dark hair on his chest. Her husband, so peacefully asleep moments before, rumbled to life like a latent volcano.

"Come back to bed, sweetheart," he coaxed, stretching forth a sinewy arm. His smile was languid and lethal.

"But what about the beastie, my love?" she demurred.

"Lass, ye have a beastie of yer own now," he said lovingly.

Eyeing the great, black-eyed giant who had won her heart, Felicity was moved to agree. She returned to bed with alacrity.

Harlequin Regency Romance™

COMING NEXT MONTH

#61 A CHELTENHAM COMEDY by Margaret Westhaven
Miss Leonora Clare fled to Cheltenham to preserve her reputation, only to fall in love with Mr. Richard Forrester, a man cloaked in mystery, whose scandalous behaviour led to the most interesting results!

#62 CUPID AND THE VICAR by Judith Stafford
Who better to play Cupid than a servant of the Lord? So Daniel Fenton believed when his younger sister, Serena, came to live with him at the vicarage. His secret desire was to see her wed to his greatest friend, Marcus Browne, Earl of Granville, though he had no way of knowing another Cupid was aiming a similar arrow at his own heart.

Take 4 bestselling love stories FREE

Plus get a FREE surprise gift!

WIN
CARS, TRIPS, CASH!

HARLEQUIN®
OFFICIAL SWEEPSTAKES
RULES

NO PURCHASE NECESSARY

1. To enter, complete an Official Entry Form or 3" × 5" index card by hand-printing, in plain block letters, your complete name, address, phone number and age, and mailing it to: Harlequin Fashion A Whole New You Sweepstakes, P.O. Box 9056, Buffalo, NY 14269-9056.

   No responsibility is assumed for lost, late or misdirected mail. Entries must be sent separately with first class postage affixed, and be received no later than December 31, 1991 for eligibility.

2. Winners will be selected by D.L. Blair, Inc., an independent judging organization whose decisions are final, in random drawings to be held on January 30, 1992 in Blair, NE at 10:00 a.m. from among all eligible entries received.

3. The prizes to be awarded and their approximate retail values are as follows: Grand Prize — A brand-new Mercury Sable LS plus a trip for two (2) to Paris, including round-trip air transportation, six (6) nights hotel accommodation, a $1,400 meal/spending money stipend and $2,000 cash toward a new fashion wardrobe (approximate value: $28,000) or $15,000 cash; two (2) Second Prizes — A trip to Paris, including round-trip air transportation, six (6) nights hotel accommodation, a $1,400 meal/spending money stipend and $2,000 cash toward a new fashion wardrobe (approximate value: $11,000) or $5,000 cash; three (3) Third Prizes — $2,000 cash toward a new fashion wardrobe. All prizes are valued in U.S. currency. Travel award air transportation is from the commercial airport nearest winner's home. Travel is subject to space and accommodation availability, and must be completed by June 30, 1993. Sweepstakes offer is open to residents of the U.S. and Canada who are 21 years of age or older as of December 31, 1991, except residents of Puerto Rico, employees and immediate family members of Torstar Corp., its affiliates, subsidiaries, and all agencies, entities and persons connected with the use, marketing, or conduct of this sweepstakes. All federal, state, provincial, municipal and local laws apply. Offer void wherever prohibited by law. Taxes and/or duties, applicable registration and licensing fees, are the sole responsibility of the winners. Any litigation within the province of Quebec respecting the conduct and awarding of a prize may be submitted to the Régie des loteries et courses du Québec. All prizes will be awarded; winners will be notified by mail. No substitution of prizes is permitted.

4. Potential winners must sign and return any required Affidavit of Eligibility/Release of Liability within 30 days of notification. In the event of noncompliance within this time period, the prize may be awarded to an alternate winner. Any prize or prize notification returned as undeliverable may result in the awarding of that prize to an alternate winner. By acceptance of their prize, winners consent to use of their names, photographs or their likenesses for purposes of advertising, trade and promotion on behalf of Torstar Corp. without further compensation. Canadian winners must correctly answer a time-limited arithmetical question in order to be awarded a prize.

5. For a list of winners (available after 3/31/92), send a separate stamped, self-addressed envelope to: Harlequin Fashion A Whole New You Sweepstakes, P.O. Box 4694, Blair, NE 60009.

PREMIUM OFFER TERMS

To receive your gift, complete the Offer Certificate according to directions. Be certain to enclose the required number of "Fashion A Whole New You" proofs of product purchase (which are found on the last page of every specially marked "Fashion A Whole New You" Harlequin or Silhouette romance novel). Requests must be received no later than December 31, 1991. Limit: four (4) gifts per name, family, group, organization or address. Items depicted are for illustrative purposes only and may not be exactly as shown. Please allow 6 to 8 weeks for receipt of order. Offer good while quantities of gifts last. In the event an ordered gift is no longer available, you will receive a free, previously unpublished Harlequin or Silhouette book for every proof of purchase you have submitted with your request, plus a refund of the postage and handling charge you have included. Offer good in the U.S. and Canada only.

HQFW-SWPR

HARLEQUIN® OFFICIAL
SWEEPSTAKES ENTRY FORM

4-FWRGS-3

Complete and return this Entry Form immediately – the more entries you submit, the better your chances of winning!

- Entries must be received by **December 31, 1991.**
- A Random draw will take place on **January 30, 1992.**
- No purchase necessary.

Yes, I want to win a FASHION A WHOLE NEW YOU Classic and Romantic prize from Harlequin:

Name _____ Telephone _____ Age _____

Address _____

City _____ State _____ Zip _____

Return Entries to: **Harlequin FASHION A WHOLE NEW YOU,**
P.O. Box 9056, Buffalo, NY 14269-9056   © 1991 Harlequin Enterprises Limited

PREMIUM OFFER

To receive your free gift, send us the required number of proofs-of-purchase from any specially marked FASHION A WHOLE NEW YOU Harlequin or Silhouette Book with the Offer Certificate properly completed, plus a check or money order (do not send cash) to cover postage and handling payable to Harlequin FASHION A WHOLE NEW YOU Offer. We will send you the specified gift.

OFFER CERTIFICATE

Item	A. ROMANTIC COLLECTOR'S DOLL (Suggested Retail Price $60.00)	B. CLASSIC PICTURE FRAME (Suggested Retail Price $25.00)
# of proofs-of-purchase	18	12
Postage and Handling	$3.50	$2.95
Check one	☐	☐

Name _____

Address _____

City _____ State _____ Zip _____

Mail this certificate, designated number of proofs-of-purchase and check or money order for postage and handling to: **Harlequin FASHION A WHOLE NEW YOU Gift Offer,** P.O. Box 9057, Buffalo, NY 14269-9057. Requests must be received by December 31, 1991.

ONE
PROOF-OF-PURCHASE

4-FWRGP-3

To collect your fabulous free gift you must include the necessary number of proofs-of-purchase with a properly completed Offer Certificate.

© 1991 Harlequin Enterprises Limited

See previous page for details.